TIME FLIES

WHEN YOU'RE CHASING SPIES

A HALIFAX MYSTERY

ALLISON MAHER

NIMBUS
PUBLISHING

For Nancy Ainsworth and Davis Keeler,
my partners in crime.

Nimbus Publishing Limited
3731 Mackintosh St, Halifax, NS B3K 5A5
(902) 455-4286 nimbus.ca

Printed and bound in Canada

Design: Tangerine Sky Designs
Author photo: Tiffany Cogswell

This novel is a work of fiction. Names, characters, places, and incidents are
either the product of the author's imagination or are used fictitiously.

Library and Archives Canada Cataloguing in Publication

Maher, Allison, 1967-
Time flies when you're chasing spies :
a Halifax mystery / Allison Maher.

Issued also in electronic format.
ISBN 978-1-55109-929-3

I. Title.
PS8626.A417T56 2012   jC813'.6   C2012-903652-8

  NOVA SCOTIA
Canada Council Conseil des arts
for the Arts du Canada
Communities, Culture and Heritage

Nimbus Publishing acknowledges the financial support for its
publishing activities from the Government of Canada through the
Canada Book Fund (CBF) and the Canada Council for the Arts, and from
the Province of Nova Scotia through the Department of Communities,
Culture, and Heritage.

CHAPTER 1

"Dad, where's Mom?" I holler up the basement stairs in frustration.

"Still at work, I guess. Why?" he calls back from the kitchen.

I would have gone up to the kitchen to ask him rather than holler, but Dad in the kitchen is always a bit frightening. Retired biochemists should never try to cook. Especially for loved ones. There ought to be a rule. Some legal paper they should sign to protect the hearts, minds, tongues, and digestive tracts of their families. It's not that his cooking usually tastes bad, it's that he knows too much about the plants in the backyard and has a naturally curious, research-based mind.

Pine needles, for example, might be really high in vitamin C and are probably really good for me. Apparently, they even grow freely on the tree beside the back deck. Dad spied them out the kitchen window and thought they'd add an authentic "woodsy" flavour to his beef and mushroom stew, but in the end they made the stew taste like one of the cleaning fluids from under the sink. Mom and I didn't want to hurt his feelings, so we ate it anyway.

"You can eat anything if you're hungry enough," Grandpa used to say. That's probably true, but I've found out the hard way that you'll eat anything if you're polite enough, too.

Knowing Dad is in the kitchen trying to brew something up for supper tonight really isn't helping me with my frustration over my mother's job. I much prefer it when she cooks, but for the past two weeks Mom's been at work more hours than she's been home.

Even when she *is* home, she's either sleeping or distracted. It's no use trying to talk to her. Her whole mind is stuck on work and the G8 summit that's coming to town.

G8 summits are some of the most important meetings that ever take place. The leaders of the world's eight most powerful countries meet and talk about all the things that are affecting the world. Money, oil, food, diseases, war, and peace are all on the list of things that need to be worked on and figured out. This year they've chosen Halifax, Nova Scotia, as the location for their meeting. It's a really big deal.

The company Mom works for, Epsom Electronics, is the electronic version of Santa's workshop for the

CIA, the FBI, the LMNOP, and any other sets of letters that mean "spy agency." All the super-sneaky people on the good guy's side of the spy world call Mom and give her their little wish lists for the year. And if they are good little boys and girls, Epsom Electronics, and Mom, will find a way to make their little spy dreams come true.

Epsom has the usual stuff that most of the spy goods manufacturers make, like cellphone-tracking systems, car- or people-tracking stuff, and microphones and cameras that you can hide in the button of a coat or whatever. Most of the time, customers just buy that stuff, but sometimes the people who show up at Mom's store need something special.

They ask for things like a face-recognition system that can be set up in the back seat of a thousand city cabs, with a cellphone system attached to each one and a connection to every police computer in the world. The idea is that every time someone gets into a taxi in, say, New York City, there will be a camera that takes a picture of their face, scans it, and sends it out to a waiting computer at every police agency in the world. The computers at those police departments can then compare the face to the faces of criminals they have on file. If there is no match, the camera turns off and nothing happens.

But if the face in the back seat is the same as the face of a wanted person in Germany, the computer in Germany has three choices. It can alert the NYPD that they can decide to just ignore the passenger, because he's a little baby criminal and not worth the gas to go pick him up. Or it might tell the NYPD the guy in the back seat is a medium-sized bad guy. Worth picking up, but not to worry because he's just naughty, not dangerous. If the guy in the back seat *is* dangerous, the German computer will skip the NYPD and call the National Guard or a SWAT unit right away. It could even tell them to send heavily armed tanks, boys in body armour, and an assault helicopter for backup.

This year, Epsom Electronics has been hired to organize the security for all the important people coming to the G8 summit—no expense spared, all the bells and whistles. My mom is the one in charge of making it all work smoothly. She's the one who figures out where to put the bells and who blows the whistles. For the past two weeks, unless I ask her how the alarm transmitters and face scanners are coming, there's been no point in opening my mouth. She just doesn't hear me.

Dad calls it "focused." I call it "annoying."

She's working late again today, and to top it off, she's changed the password on her home computer. I can't get on it to print off my homework assignment, and it's due tomorrow.

It would be one thing if I could just tell the teacher, "Sorry. My mom has been a little preoccupied trying to keep all the world leaders safe, so her high-tech, space-age computer ate my homework." But I can't do that, because everyone thinks her company makes bird-tracking stuff for the Department of the Environment. No one outside the police world is allowed to know what she really does.

I've spent my whole life lying about it. It comes quite naturally to me now. The only person I don't have to lie to about it is my best friend, Brian. He understands my need for secrets. He hasn't spent his whole life lying about his mother, but he, on the other hand, has spent the past three years lying to the world about who *he* is. Brian and his family are in the Witness Protection Program. They've ended up here, because it was cheaper to set his family up in rural Nova Scotia, Canada, than it would have been to set them up in Paris, France. Not to mention the fact that they don't speak a word of French.

Right now, standing at the bottom of the stairs, I could scream in frustration. I squeeze the handrail instead and decide to drop it. I'll just go hang out with Brian. He's at least good for a laugh. "Dad, I'm going to Brian's to see if I can get at my homework from there," I call up the stairs.

"You can't hack into Mom's computer and you know it," he calls down to me. He doesn't sound annoyed, just sympathetic. "You know as well as I do that even your mom can't hack into her own computer from off-site, and she at least has the password. But have fun anyway," Dad says. Then words to nightmare by: "Supper will be ready around seven, so don't be late. Tell Brian I'll take you guys for another driving session this weekend if you want."

Brian and I are both thirteen and just bought our first dirt bikes. Our parents thought that if we were busy driving around on dirt bikes it might keep us out of trouble. Either that or it was a new hobby for Dad. He's the one showing us the ropes. Driving lessons with Dad are way better than suppers with Dad. He's teaching us how to do emergency brake skids. His theory is that if he teaches us how to come out of a controlled slide, then we'll have a better chance of making it out of an accidental one. We won't panic and we'll know what to do. It's good fun.

I sigh and leave through the back door. Brian's house is only a ten-minute walk away, but now that I have a dirt bike, I drive anyway. Sometimes life is sweet!

CHAPTER 2

"Is Mom home yet?" I ask loudly the very second my toe comes in the front door. Irritation is mounting. I had been hoping she would be home and I'd be able to get on her computer, but really I knew she wasn't home the minute I pulled in to the yard. Mom's modified car with all the extra wires and antennas wasn't in its usual spot.

"No," Dad answers with a bit of a sigh. He fires his tea towel in the direction of the counter without even looking where it might land as he steps into the front hallway through the archway that leads to the living room off to the right. "I've called her twice already and she hasn't answered or returned my calls. I'll try her again to see if I should hold supper a little longer or if we should just eat without her."

Dad is one of the calmest people on the planet. I've only seen him lose his cool twice in my life, both over major events. To see him even slightly out of sorts makes me step back a little and decide that perhaps I should cool it on being annoyed with Mom.

I hang the bike keys back up on the hook where they belong and take off my shoes as Dad picks up the cordless from the hall table, punches in her cellphone number, turns away from me, and heads for the kitchen at the far end of the hall.

"Humph," he says, staring at the face of the phone. "Straight to voicemail."

"Try her office," I offer as I start towards the kitchen behind him. "If she's still there, someone else might be too."

Dad punches in a new set of numbers. "Hi, Jack," he says into the phone. "Is Marion around? I think her cell must be turned off."

I move towards the cupboard and start getting plates to set the table. Dad doesn't follow me. He stops in the middle of the kitchen floor.

"Marion's not sick," he says with a touch of confusion. "She hasn't been home all day."

I try not to rattle the dishes, and move slowly so as not to make any noise. I try hard to listen. Dad still doesn't move from his spot on the floor. He says nothing for a while.

"All right," he finally says into the phone. "Let me know when you track her down. We'll both have to give her the devil for not keeping in touch. Thanks, Jack." He pulls the phone away from his ear slowly and clicks the button to hang it up.

"Your mother hasn't been at work all afternoon. They thought she must be home sick," Dad tells me distractedly. He dials her cell number again and presses the phone to his ear. "They're going to call the airport and the Citadel to see where she is," he says to me without making eye contact. "If she's not here or at the office, she must be at either of those places. She's probably doing some last-minute checks on equipment."

I stop arranging dishes on the table. He hangs up the phone without speaking. He doesn't have to tell me the call went to voicemail again. The cords bulge in my father's neck and his eyes flick unseeingly, left and right. He is deep in thought. I can almost see him hunting for Mom in his mind.

"Dad," I try to interrupt his thoughts, but it doesn't register. I try again a little louder. "Dad. We can track her car."

There's a pause while he looks at me. He studies me. I know he doesn't want me to worry.

"Mom's always testing stuff. Look at her office in the basement. It's full of stuff."

His eyes narrow as he thinks about what I'm saying.

"Her car is no different," I continue. "There's

always some new transmitter or something on her car that she's testing, right? All we have to do is go downstairs and see what's *not* there, and we can figure out which piece of gear she was testing last. It's probably still in the trunk or under the bumper. If we know what she has in the car, we can just go find her. She's got plenty of receivers in the basement. Right?" I ask hopefully.

I've spent most of my life as Mom's test subject. She's forever testing spy gear at home. Sometimes she needs me to take a transmitter and hide it in the neighbourhood so she can try to find it. Sometimes *she* hides the transmitter and asks me to try to find it with a new tracking system she's testing. That way she can see what mistakes a customer might make with it. It helps her train others how to use Epsom Electronics' stuff.

"No," Dad says calmly. He starts moving again. "They'll call in a few minutes and let us know where she is." He walks to the cupboard and picks up a stack of plates as he's talking, then heads to the dining room table. Looking down at the table, he freezes with plates in hand, staring down at the table I've just finished setting.

"They'll call any minute," he repeats as he returns to the kitchen to put the unnecessary plates away.

"Let's eat. I've made your favourite."

"Pepperoni and cheese pizza?" I ask. We both know it's not. I'm just trying to lighten the mood.

"Almost," he says, lifting the lid off the cast-iron pot on the stove. "How about shepherd's pie?" He smiles and uses his free hand to display his latest creation for me.

"Is there a shepherd in it?" I ask, raising my eyebrows and peeking over the rim of the pot nervously.

"No," he laughs, and ruffles my hair.

"So what *is* in it that you're not telling me about?"

"Burdocks," he states.

I'm silent for a moment. I know he's not joking. "You mean those spiky little balls that get stuck in my pant leg, or some other kind of burdock?" I ask hopefully.

"No," he grins at me. "They're the same ones that get stuck in your pants, but I didn't use the seed pods, I used the roots. Mom asked me to weed out around the back fence, so I figured why not? I think it'll taste okay," he adds with a reinforcing nod of his head.

We both lean in for a sniff. It smells fine. Way better than the pine needles did. Dad raises his eyebrows, silently asking me if I'm willing to give it a try. I nod my head and he starts to scoop.

The phone rings. Immediately Dad stops scooping, puts the half-filled plate down on the counter with a rattle, and snatches up the phone.

"Marion?" he asks quickly. His voice drops as he mentally pulls back. "Hi, Jack...No, she hasn't called all afternoon...Not there either, eh? You tell me, Jack. Should I be worried?" Dad turns his back to me. He starts walking out of the kitchen towards the basement stairs. "Andrew had a good idea earlier. He suggested we take an inventory of the basement to figure out what she's got on her and just track her down ourselves."

I follow him as he heads down the stairs and into Mom's office in the basement. Dad looks around at the shelves of books, folders, and electronic bits and pieces.

"You see what you can find from your end," he says into the phone. "And Jack. We need speed." Dad hangs up.

"What is it, Dad?" I can see he's not happy. The look on his face is making me nervous.

The phone rings before he can answer me.

"Marion?" he barks into the phone. Dad rolls his eyes and hangs his head slightly. He looks annoyed. "Oh, hello," he says with a voice like a balloon with all the air being let out at once. He listens for a second, then interrupts the person on the other end. "Mr. MacDonald, I'm sorry, but I'm a little busy right now. I can't really talk." Dad looks very impatient. He hangs his head farther and braces one hand on his hip. Mr. MacDonald is an old dairy farmer who makes his own cheese and sells it at the farmers' market on Saturdays. He calls Dad sometimes when he wants help changing his feed or fertilizer.

Suddenly Dad's head snaps up and he drops his hand from his hip. He turns away from the office, takes the stairs two at a time, and turns right, towards the front door. Our hunt for electronic debris is forgotten.

"No! You did right to call us!" he exclaims into the phone. "I'll be right there. Fifteen minutes max. Thank you, Mr. MacDonald!" Dad clicks off the phone and hits redial.

"Come on, Andrew," he calls over his shoulder as he starts jogging past the living room and through the front hall.

"Hello, Jack. A neighbour found her car in a field near exit thirteen." He pauses in front of the hall table to listen. I can see his face reflected in the mirror. It's a stranger's face: hard and dark. "No, she's not in the car. I'll phone you when we get there."

Dad drops the phone on the table beside the front door, grabs the keys off the hook, and heads out to the car. I'm close on his heels. I skid to a stop in front of the security control panel and push the flashing red button that turns on all the systems at once. I now have thirty seconds to get out of the house before the alarms activate, but it takes me less than five seconds to pull on my shoes, get out of the house, and shut the door behind me.

Our house has been wired up with more security systems than the local bank ever since Brian came to town and created a little chaos for us. Mom figures that if she works for a high-end electronics company, someone out there at least owes her an obscenely good security system. Her boss agrees and now you can't come within thirty feet of our house without setting off ten alarms or having your picture taken and sent to God.

Normally I ignore the alarm system, except when I set it off by accident. But for some reason, right now, it makes me feel better.

I sprint to the car and slide into the front seat just as Dad drops the car into reverse and squeals the tires the full length of the driveway. My head snaps around and I'm pulled a few inches across the seat as Dad whips the wheel to the left, swinging the nose of the car around to face down the street. He drops the transmission from reverse to drive before the wheels have stopped spinning and sliding. Black smoke billows up around the back of the car as we skid sideways for a brief second. Then the tires find traction with the cement and the car begins to race forward. The back of the car fishtails behind us as we gain speed on our narrow suburban street.

That'll get the neighbours talking, I think to myself as the engine roars. Dad has his foot planted on the gas pedal, pressing it hard to the floor. At the end of our street, he lifts his foot long enough to crank the wheel and have us skid sideways around the corner and through the intersection.

Dad zigs around whatever can be zigged around, and zags around the rest. We rocket out of town. It's early evening and the streets are almost empty. The highway is mostly clear of cars too, as we turn onto the on-ramp and race past two exits to exit thirteen. Dad barely slows the car at all as he pulls off the highway and speeds towards our destination.

We don't speak until I spot the car. I don't actually see it right away. Instead, I see one of the radio-frequency antennas. There are four of them, but it takes me a split second to see the other three. They all stick straight up, about two feet above the roof of the car. I can see them above the tops of the tall stalks of ryegrass in the middle of a field ahead.

"Over there, Dad!" I yell above the roar of the engine, breaking our silence, my hand pointing into the vast field. "That's her car! Look at the antennas!"

The field is a solid wall of tall grass. We need to figure out how she got her car in there and how we can get our car in there too.

Black marks on the road ahead give us the answer. It looks like mom locked up her brakes, then cranked her wheel hard, towards the ditch. It looks like she corrected the vehicle just before it hit the shoulder.

I look into the field for a clue. A few feet farther, a path opens up in the grass where mom drove over it. You can see the crushed grass where the tires went and the slightly raised grass where the body of the car passed over and bent it, but didn't crush it.

Dad swerves the car and aims it in the direction I've just pointed. The tires leave the pavement and make a popping-crunching sound as they cross over the gravel at the side of the road. Luckily, the ditch is almost level with the road. The car jumps a little as it enters the ditch, then bounces, the springs grinding and clunking in protest as we thunder through the field. The tall stalks of ryegrass whip and slap against the side of the car, making loud thwacking sounds. I'm catching glimpses of the antennas, so we know we're getting closer.

Rounding a slight curve in the path, we see the car. Dad hits the brakes hard. The tires lock under the car and we slide in the dirt and grass like a giant steel bobsled. Far too quickly, we come to a stop.

My body is thrown forward enough that the seat belt catches and holds me tight, pressing into my chest. I put both my hands out and brace myself against the dash. We're thirty feet behind her back bumper. It's further away than I thought we would stop. I'm slightly confused, but say nothing. We both jump out and run to the car.

"Don't touch anything," Dad advises. "You might interfere with the evidence." He pauses.

"What do you see?"

We both head for the driver's side of the car and survey the ground for prints and tracks. There are plenty. No plants can compete with fast-growing grasses, so there is nothing but fluffy black soil beneath the rye stalks. The prints are easy to see.

The top prints are from broad rubber boots. The stance is fairly far apart, about shoulder width, a sign of an older person. The right toe leaves a long drag mark before the toe finally clears the ground for the next step—this person has a bit of a limp, so these are probably Mr. MacDonald's prints. He must have walked up to the car when he found it to see if he could help.

Below his prints is a strange design. It looks like someone tried to draw a set of train tracks in the loose soil. There are two lines in the dirt. They aren't an equal distance apart. The space between the lines gets wider and narrower in places. There are big footprints along both sides of the lines.

I can see what has happened here like a movie playing in my head. It's a scary movie that grips my throat and stops my breath.

Mom had high heels on when she went to work this morning. Someone walked up to her door in this field and opened it. She stepped out and then someone dragged my mother away from her car. Her heels digging into the soil made these prints. She was refusing to walk, or at least doing her best not to be helpful. As we follow the tracks I can see where she resisted. The straight, scraping lines her heels made stop abruptly, and there is a cluster of twenty or thirty prints all in a jumble.

Some of them, I can see clearly, are from a pair of high heels.

I can see where Mom tried to pull back, step away, and throw her attacker off balance. She didn't stand a chance. Where she resisted, the footprints are all mixed up, but a few inches further down the trail of footprints, I can see clearly there is an extra set of tracks; now there's one on either side of my mother's dragging heels.

They are big and deep. There doesn't seem to be any tread or pattern. Expensive men's dress shoes often have smooth leather soles. You don't need good, deep treads on your shoes if you never plan on wearing them outside of an office with plush carpeting.

The men who took my mother were big, probably both over six feet—I can tell by the huge distance between their footprints. They aren't running strides, either; the heel impressions aren't deeper than the toes. They were probably wearing suits. Only men in suits would be wearing smooth-soled dress shoes. I can see it all in my mind's eye and the picture keeps getting worse. My mother was trapped between two giants in suits.

Without warning, my stomach empties its contents into the tall grain field. I fall to my knees and continue to heave. My mind spins in disbelief. All these years, Mom had worried about security and the safety of our family and I had ignored her warnings. Countless times I had teased her about being paranoid, and now she was gone. Taken away from us. We hadn't even known it was happening.

My father has been reading the tracks beside me. He's the one who taught me how to read them. We both know what these tracks mean. He doesn't have to tell me.

I hear him speaking into his cellphone behind me. With one hand on the phone, he touches my shoulder gently with his free hand. I wipe my lips with the back of my hand and stand on shaky legs. Dad starts back for our car, guiding me with him. I pull out of his grasp and run to the closed door on the passenger side of my mother's abandoned car. There wouldn't be any prints for the police to find on the passenger side door, so I grab it and practically rip the door off its hinges as the adrenaline in my body kicks into high gear.

Fear can make you really strong and really fast. I can feel my pulse beating in my fingertips. It makes my hair stand on end.

I climb into the passenger side and drive my hand under the seat, fishing around for her purse, her wallet, anything. There is nothing but empty fast food wrappers and disposable coffee cups. Lurching forward, I give a quick sweep under the driver seat. Nothing there, either. My heart screams with relief. I climb backwards and out of the car, scrambling on my hands and knees, slamming the door shut with more force than it needs.

Dad is standing in the open door of his car, a look of expectation on his face.

"Purse is gone," I announce with a surge of hope.

"She has her phone with her. It's a place to start," I yell at him as I run towards his waiting car.

He gives me a quick nod. "Good thinking," he tells me, tossing me his phone over the hood of the car. "You call Jack back and tell him what to look for, and I'll drive." He smiles and adds, "My shepherd's pie would have smelled a whole lot better coming up than those Doritos did."

CHAPTER 3

We jump into the car. Dad drives like a madman while I dial my mother's boss. The secretaries all leave at six and it's now at least quarter after. Jack answers the phone himself on the first ring.

"Please tell me you have good news," he says without a formal hello.

I'm shocked for a moment as I realize that my mother has been taken by someone and I'm about to talk to my mother's boss about it. I'm not calling to tell him she won't be in for work this afternoon because she has a cold. I'm calling her in *kidnapped*.

"Yes," I say. "The good news is, she still has her purse on her." I stop speaking because I don't trust my voice.

Jack understands, without me having to say the words, that she is gone.

"I've got her cell number. We'll start linking up to the satellites and the cell towers right away. I promise, Andrew, we'll have something for you by the time you get here." His voice is full of authority. Jack is a man who is used to getting things done.

I'm glad he's on my side.

Twenty minutes later, Dad swerves into the parking lot where my mother works and skids to a stop at the front door. He doesn't park, he just shuts the car off and jumps out.

Jack is at the door waiting for us. He shows us through.

Inside, the offices and factory look a little messier than usual. Everyone seems to be talking and walking around with a cup of coffee in one hand and either a piece of electronics or a piece of paper in the other. They nod politely as we storm past.

"What have you got, Jack?" Dad asks sharply.

"Her phone was turned off. Maritime Telephone agreed to get the cell towers to send out the signal that turns on her phone. It will wake up partway and start transmitting, but none of the lights will come on and it won't ring. We'll start to use other towers to find out where the phone is. If we think it's safe, we can turn the phone on all the way and just call her. But if the phone is off, which Marion's phone *never* is, it's deliberate. She's telling us something."

Dad and Jack are striding so fast, I practically have to jog to keep up. The water cooler almost takes me out as we round the corner towards the main offices.

"Marion is a smart cookie. She knows not to alert whoever took her to the fact she has a phone. If the phone rings or they otherwise notice it, they'll take if from her and either throw it away or turn it off. If they throw it away, we're sunk. If they just turn it off, we're still in business. We can turn on any cell phone in the world, wherever it is, without anyone knowing about it. Then we can start asking the cell towers to search for the phone, just as if they were going to call it."

Just past the offices, we head up the staircase that lead to the roof. I take the stairs two at a time.

"When you dial someone's cell number, the towers start looking for that phone within their area of responsibility. They know in less time than it takes you to blink whether the phone is within their reach. If it is not, they tell the next tower out to start looking. The cell towers talk to one another very quickly. In the time it takes for the phone to ring twice, every cell tower in North America could have searched for that phone."

The three of us are stopped at the landing at the top of the stairs, in front of the Plexiglas door that leads to the testing dome at the top of the building.

It is a very space-age-looking room, like half of a ball sitting on the roof. A dome made out of tinted glass and plastic panels.

Jack opens the door to the testing dome. A small buzzer sounds, and a few people turn around to look at us. They nod and turn back to whatever they're doing. Their faces are serious and unsmiling. Jack closes the door behind us. The loud buzzing stops.

"We've got Devon, our computer genius, set up for this at the back there," he says, using his hand in a sweeping motion to let us know where to go. We follow Jack past several workstations with more buttons, toggles, antennas, and wires than the bridge of the Starship *Enterprise*.

We stop by a sweaty bald man with a wireless earpiece who's typing furiously. I guess he must be Devon.

"The guys in the lab should be getting something from the towers by now," Jack explains to us, then turns to Devon. "What have you got on her so far?"

"She's still in Nova Scotia," he tells us with a reassuring nod and a glance over his shoulder.

I don't feel reassured. It made me realize for the first time that someone might be trying to take her outside of the province. I get a full-body shiver, even though it's warm in the room.

"We've got two cell towers picking up her phone already and they're both between the airport and Halifax. She's still moving, but with only one or two towers on line, we can't say for sure where she's moving to, or how fast she's getting there."

"Why do we care how fast she's going?" I ask. "If you have some idea where she is, why don't you just send the police to go get her?"

"Her speed will help us tell the police what to send to go get her," Devon explains over his shoulder, still typing furiously. "If she's only moving five k.p.h., then we know they're on foot, and we'll tell them to send tracking dogs. If she's moving fifty k.p.h., then we know she's in a vehicle and tell them to send a car or a four-by-four. But neither of those are going to do us any good if she's moving five hundred k.p.h., because that means she's in an airplane and the dogs and cars might as well just stay home."

I feel stupid. I really should have known that.

"Cellphones don't work in airplanes, do they?" I ask, trying to recover.

"They work *great* from airplanes," he tells me. "You're just not supposed to use them because they could interfere with the pilot's computer system. The reception is great up there. Cell towers can't tell if they're looking up or down. Even if your mother is in an airplane, we still need the third tower to give us a signal strength reading before we can put her on a map, either on the ground, or in the air."

Dad, who hasn't heard this a million times from mom, looks confused, and Devon elaborates as he types.

"Imagine a cell tower as a person standing in a parking lot. When a cell phone calls them, that person can't see the phone, but can tell the phone is twenty feet away by how loud the ring is. The cell tower person can then take a bucket full of water with a hole in the bottom and tie it to a piece of rope that is twenty feet long. When the cell tower person swings the bucket around their head in a great big circle, it will leave a circle of water in the parking lot. Somewhere on the water circle is the cell phone. That makes for a lot of area to cover.

"A second person walks into the parking lot and hears the phone ringing. They know the phone is five feet away, so they take a bucket full of water with a hole in the bottom and tie it to a five-foot rope. When they swing their rope in a circle, it will also spill water in a perfect circle marking the ground. If the phone is five feet away, it must be somewhere on that line.

"Those two circles of water will overlap in two places, just like two hula hoops thrown on the ground, one on top of the other. If you want to find the phone, you now have only two places to look.

"Now if a third person comes into the parking lot and hears the phone and swings his bucket of water, there will only be one place in the whole parking lot where all three water lines cross one another. And that place is exactly where you'll find the phone."

In my mother's case, they aren't in a parking lot, they're in an entire province. I watch as Devon types as fast as I can read. He flips screens so fast I can't keep track of what he's looking for.

"Third tower reporting in," Devon tells us as he tips his head toward the computer screen, typing away. His head flicks up and down from the keys to the screen. The monitor blinks up with a map of Nova Scotia and zooms in on the centre of the province. Three bright blue circles flash onto the screen. When they vanish, a blinking blue dot stays on the screen where the three circles crossed each other.

"We've got her," announces Devon in a big voice.

My heart leaps in relief and fear at the same time. If only I could step through the screen and be where that dot is.

Devon leans over to poke the number keys on the side of his keyboard. "Staff Sergeant Herron, please," he says as if to one of us in the room, but I realize his computer is patched into the telephone system, and he has dialled police headquarters. With his eyes darting around his workstation, he continues to flick levers and strike keys.

"Staff Sergeant Herron?" Devon asks into thin air. "We've got our girl. From here on we'll give her the code name Petal." There is a brief silence for the rest of us in the room. Devon turns his head to adjust another knob off to his side and I see a small skin-coloured blob hiding in his ear. It's the earpiece to his telephone.

"Petal is on the move," he continues. "Petal is between exit two and exit three on Highway 102 heading north, away from Halifax and towards both the airport and the provincial border. We'll remain radio silent until you have men in place, or we feel there is a change of route…Good to go." Devon strikes a key sharply to disconnect the call. "The cavalry is on its way," he says after swivelling in his seat. "Now all we can do is sit and wait."

"That's not really something my family does very well," I tell him as I spin on my heel and head back out the way we came in.

CHAPTER 4

"Andrew," Dad says to me as we pull up to the curb outside our house. "You're thirteen years old. You are too young to be involved in this, but I know if I tell you to go home and wait, you won't do it."

"No. I won't," I confirm with a surge of anger. I all but dare him to tell me to stay out of this.

"So I'll ask you this. Call Brian. His parents are out of town and can't be reached. We don't know what these people know about us, and it's conceivable they could go after Brian too. Get him out of his house. The two of you need to grab what you can out of the basement and get a cab for the airport."

Dad pulls out his wallet while he's talking and hands me sixty bucks. "Try to look like a tourist. These guys will be expecting the police, not a couple of kids who look like they're heading off for their first vacation. Look for anything suspicious. Look for your mother. The best place to hide someone is in plain sight. If you find something, don't do anything, just call Jack or me. Wherever you are in the airport, we won't be far away."

"You're telling me to get involved?" I ask with shock.

"Not if I want to live more than ten seconds once we find your mother," he says with a smile. The smile fades as quickly as it appeared and he adds, "I love your mother and I love you. Right now I would dance with the devil himself if I though that would help to get her back. You've grown up in a world of spies and electronics and figuring out how to out-think the other guy, anticipate his next move and get ahead of him. I need you. Your mother needs you. But we're going to work with the authorities, okay?"

"Okay," I say, feeling very humble. My father is putting so much faith in me.

"We need to keep in touch here, both of us. I'm heading back to the office. If we get any clues that she's moved or isn't stopping at the airport, I'll call."

We exchange a smile and I pull the handle to the door and step out of the car.

"Son?" he says as I step away from the door about to close it.

"Yes, Dad?" I say bending over to see him in the car.

"Stay safe."

I nod and shut the door. I have to blink back the wetness in my eyes. I'm proud that Dad thinks I can help and I'm determined to help find my mother. I'm also over-the-top afraid we won't find her in time. In time for what? I don't know, but I do know this: time flies when you're chasing spies.

I don't watch as he leaves, but I hear the tires squeal as they spin on the surface of the road before the car picks up enough speed to catch up to the wheels.

I call Brian and tell him what has happened. Any other person in the world would have thought I was pulling their leg. They would have laughed or called a psychiatrist, but not Brian. We've been through this kind of thing before.

The reason city-slicker Brian even lives in teeny-tiny Aylesford is because the Witness Protection Program plunked his whole family down in our neighbourhood. I made friends with him before we found out the whole family was in hiding. They didn't hide very well, though; the mob ended up finding them and burning down their house. If it hadn't been for Brian and me fooling around with Mom's tracking equipment, we never would have gotten Brian and his family back from the mob. Usually the Witness Protection Program moves families far, far away if they're found, but in this case, they just moved Brian close, close to Mom. They bought him and his parents the house across the street from us. They NEVER do stuff like that, which is exactly why they did it. That and mom agreed to be their electronic watchdog.

Brian is on his way before I end the call. Moments later, he rounds the corner of his house and appears on the lawn across the street. I walk towards him. The closer he gets, the better I feel. He's almost exactly my age, except instead of having my blond hair and blue eyes; he has dark brown hair and brown eyes. I'm an inch or two taller than he is, but he outweighs me by thirty pounds. Brian started out a little chubby in his younger years. He discovered girls and push-ups at the exact same moment, and now, most of his chub is turning into muscles. He still has a little fluff around his middle, but he could out-arm-wrestle anyone I know.

I meet up with him at the edge of his lawn and we walk back towards my house together. I fill him in as much as possible. We play a quick game of question and answer. Both of us have lots of questions, but neither of us has any answers.

We both automatically stop at the edge of my family's walkway. Once you cross over onto our lawn you only have so many seconds before the alarm starts talking to you. It scared the life out of the paperboy the first few times he walked up to the house and the house alarm asked him, in a stern electronic voice, to identify himself. As an added bonus, we never get any door-to-door sales calls.

By some unspoken agreement, I join Brian and we hurry to the door together. I punch in the code on the keypad beside the door and turn the handle. In three big strides I am through the front hall and past the living room door. Brian shuts the door behind us as I head to the basement office.

The front door closes about the time I walk into the kitchen. It's dusk outside and although it seemed light enough with the big front door open, with it closed, the kitchen seems a little dark. I flick on the light as I turn down the basement stairs.

The light doesn't come on. *Odd*, I think. My brain kicks into high gear, instantly searching for clues.

The alarm didn't beep to let me know it was turned off either, I realize. I freeze with one foot on the top step and the other in mid-air.

I listen.

Nothing. There are no house sounds. The fridge isn't humming. The air conditioner isn't making tiny clicking noises and the ceiling fan isn't turning. The ceiling fan in the kitchen is never turned off. The house is dead.

I see a shadow of movement from the hallway in the basement below me.

"Get out!" I scream back to my friend, as I spin out of the doorway. Using my arms to push myself back from the door casing and my free leg as a whip, I fly back from the opening.

In the half-light of the kitchen I sense an object fly through the space where I had just been standing. A pinging sound comes from the cupboards above the stove, quickly followed by the sound of a skipping rope falling to the floor.

Someone just tried to shoot me with a double-dart tazer gun! If it had hit me, every muscle in my body would have frozen. I would still be completely awake, I would have been able to see what was happening and hear what was being said, but I would have been completely unable to move, scream, run, or even blink.

The gun looks a bit like a dart gun, except it shoots two darts at once, and the darts are attached to long cables. The two prongs are like the + and the – on a battery. Most batteries have the + post and the – post on opposite ends. Except nine-volt batteries, which have both posts on top. If you lick the top of a nine-volt battery, your tongue will act like a wire connecting the two, completing the circuit. Your tongue will get a zap as the electricity stored in the batteries tries to travel through it to get from the + post to the – post.

With the double-dart tazer gun, once they shoot the two prongs into you, it completes the circuit and you get a continuous zap of electricity running through your body, just like the nine-volt to your tongue, except it short-circuits all your muscles. The minute the prongs are out and the extra electricity stops confusing your muscles, you go back to normal. Theoretically, no harm done.

In fact, I would be lying helpless on the kitchen floor with someone trying to hurt me.

Whoever is in the basement won't be able to shoot me with the tazer gun again until he recoils the prongs. I have at least a few seconds. Not wanting to cross in front of the opening to the basement, I run full speed through the kitchen towards the dining room. I hear the front door open and slam—Brian has made it out. At the same time, I hear feet thundering up the stairs. My attacker is making his next move. He's coming for me.

I need a diversion, something to slow him down.

Running through the kitchen, I pass the stove.

The abandoned dinner plates are still there, on the counter. I grab two and whip them back over my shoulders in the general direction of the basement stairs. There is no time to stop and aim, just to run and throw. The clunk and smash as they hit the walls and floor on the far side of the kitchen reaches my ears as I run past the dining room table and head towards the patio doors.

I grab the back of Dad's chair and use it to slingshot myself around the far end of the table. I've done it a thousand times when I've been horsing around with my friends. I pray my sneakers will grip the floor. If I were in just socks I'd be sliding on my bottom by now. Glancing over my shoulder, I grab the handle on one patio door and jerk it down.

It clicks, but the door doesn't open when I yank it. The force pulls me into the door instead of pulling the door open to me.

The lock!

My heart is pounding. Fear runs up my spine and my mouth is instantly dry.

Of course the door is locked. Panic explodes inside my head, but I fight it.

With my one hand still on the handle, I flick the bolt latch with the other. With one last look over my shoulder, I fiercely pull open the door and slam it shut again, dropping to the floor and rolling as soundlessly as possible under the dining room table.

It's my house and I'm not leaving it. They are.

The equipment I need to find my mother is in that basement.

From under the short tablecloth that covers our dining room table, I see someone walk by in men's dress shoes...with leather soles, I suspect. I move silently to a crouch under the table. I can't see the rest of the intruder from here, just his feet. Spinning on my toes, I follow him as he hurries towards the patio door.

He hesitates before he rounds the end of the table. He must be checking behind him and looking into the kitchen, just like I did. One more step and he won't be able to see the kitchen, the basement door, or the entrance to the hallway. Apparently he decides to follow me rather than go back the way he came, and starts moving again. I see his shoes moving quickly over to the patio door. Opening a door puts your body off balance. I am banking on it. I'll need the extra leverage. I hear the handle click.

Pushing off like an Olympic sprinter coming out of the blocks, I slam the full weight of my body into the backs of his knees. I had hoped he would tumble over my back, but he must still have a grip on the handle, because he tilts sideways instead of falling. I keep moving forward, bunching my feet up under me and lifting for all I'm worth to try and topple him. I grab one of his ankles with both my hands and heave.

It works!

He is far enough off balance that my extra pressure on his feet tips the scales. As his feet come off the floor, my body shoots up almost beside him. His hand smashes into the door frame as we both go spinning towards the large glass door. The glass holds for a split second then gives way with an explosive crash.

The glass of the patio doors is tempered, which makes it stronger than regular glass, but when it goes, it goes big time. Tiny crystals of glass rain down around us as we tumble out through the newly created opening in the side of my house and out onto the deck.

His shoulders hit first. He makes a grunting sound, but not "oof," like we would in English. It sounds more like "krra." My attacker is not a local.

I try to land on him, but he somehow manages to plant his foot in the middle of my chest on my way down. If feels like I've been kicked by a truck. The air leaves my lungs in a quick rush and before I know it, my feet are flipping over my head as I sail overtop of him. I miss him completely. I tuck my head in before I come pounding down on the deck, completely missing the man in the smooth-soled shoes.

I slam onto my back, the wind knocked out of me for the second time in less than five seconds. Any shred of air left in my lungs a moment ago is gone now. Pain explodes through every fibre of me as I come to a full and final stop on my back. I don't slide. I stay anchored to the wooden deck. Arching my body, I try to roll over and breathe at the same time. I can't do either.

My attacker is on me. I throw up a hand to try to deflect him, but he bats my hand away effortlessly. I'm as weak as a baby. He lands with his full weight on my chest. I almost black out, but fight it. I can see stars and the world spins around me. He says something to me but it's short and my head is spinning too much for it to register. I can feel the grip of his strong hand still pinning me by the throat. Again he barks something at me, and then tightens his grip.

My instincts are kicking in. I try to grab his arm to pull his hand away from my throat. I know I'm running out of air and I'm running out of time. Things are starting to go black. I'm passing out. Hearing is always the last of the senses to let go. I focus hard on it to try to stay with him and in control of myself, trying to stay here and not fade out.

Somewhere in the distance I hear a giant gong.

Ka-thunk!

The pressure on my throat releases. A cool dribble of air trickles down my throat and into my burning lungs. The weight bearing down on my chest changes. It slips from the centre and pushes to one side. My hands grasp at the top of my shirt, pulling it away from my airway. The weight on my chest slides off as I pull in my first real breath. It hurts going in. My lungs were screaming for air only moments ago, and now they are screaming at its arrival. Every molecule of air burns its way down my throat, into my lungs and bloodstream. My arms feel like they're on fire.

I roll onto my side and cough. The deck is sticky and wet. It doesn't smell like wood. It smells like potatoes.

"Andrew?" Brian says urgently from somewhere very close. "Come on, man! Up on your feet."

"Brian?" I croak out through my damaged throat. "Where did you come from? I heard the front door. I heard you leave!" I blink hard a few times to clear my head. I can feel his hands lifting me from under my armpits.

"I wouldn't leave without you, man," he says. "I just slammed the front door and hid in the living room for a second until I figured out what was going on. Then I heard all this noise from the dining room and thought I should come rescue you." Brian smiles at me. It's a goofy grin. He shifts his hands to steady me by the shoulders rather than hold me up by the armpits. "As soon as I came through from the kitchen, I saw that big ox holding you down by the throat and knew I had to do something."

Looking down at the deck I think I must be seeing things. There are lumps of potatoes and gravy, meat and vegetables all over the place.

"What's that?" I ask, pushing myself away from him, finding my own balance on my shaky legs.

"I think it used to be shepherd's pie," Brian answers, surveying the deck around us and trying to steer me back towards the shattered door.

Looking to the left, I see a crumpled body. It's still barely dusk, so it's lighter outside than it was inside the house, so I can easily make out the lumps of food splattered all over the deck and the back of the crumpled body's nice suit. Orange carrots and green peas go really well with black pinstripes. The cast-iron dish I saw Dad pull out of the oven a little over an hour ago now lies mostly empty on its side, a few inches from the stranger's head.

"You hit him with a casserole?" I ask stupidly.

"It's all I could find! I could have tried slapping him with a fluffy placemat, but I doubt that would have convinced him to play nice with his new friend," Brian drawls sarcastically, "seeing as he had his new friend by the throat."

I can't help but laugh as I step in through the hole that was once our patio door. Shattered glass crunches under my shoes.

Brain laughs a little too, lets go of my shoulders, and pats me on the back.

I stop halfway through the door. "Shouldn't we do something with him?" I say, jerking my head towards the man with the spoiled suit, lying in a puddle of shepherd's pie on my deck.

"What do you *want* to do with him?" Brian asks.

"I don't know." My head is mostly clear, but I'm still a little confused.

"Me neither. It's not like you can just call the local police and say, "I've got a man with a cast-iron hat napping in my backyard. Can you come get him, please?' Like the neighbours don't think you guys are weird enough. Let's just get out of here. He wasn't here to rob the place; he was here for either you or your dad. Probably to use you as a threat against your mom. You know…like in the movies, 'Do what I say, or else the kid gets it.'"

Brian and I stare at the man in the stew-covered suit for a few seconds. Anger washes over me. How dare these people kidnap my mother and then try to use me as a weapon against her?

"We should at least tie him up," I decide out loud, then step the rest of the way through the door, grab all three cloth napkins off the table, and head back out.

"You're the Boy Scout," Brain tells me, waving me off as I offer him one of the yellow napkins with blue flowers. "This operation is up to you. I'll go see if I can find a flashlight."

"Good idea," I say absentmindedly. Then I add, "before you do that, can you call Luigi's and order three six-inch pizzas with the works and a two-litre of pop? Tell them we need it delivered here as soon as possible."

"You plan on whackin' the guy with six-inch pizzas when he wakes up?" Brian asks with a shocked look on his face.

"No, he's had enough to eat already. I don't need the pizza, I need the driver. Dad wasn't thinking clearly when he dropped me off. He gave me sixty bucks and told me to get a cab to the airport, but that won't even get us halfway there. Danny drives for Luigi, and they can't be that busy on a Tuesday night. I'm hoping I can talk him into taking the long way back to the pizza shop for a forty-dollar tip and free six-inch. That'll leave one for you and one for me."

"Man, you are sneaky," he says with pride and heads into the house. I can vaguely hear him make the call.

My head is clear as I squat beside the man and stick my fingers against his neck, just under his jaw, to check for breathing and a pulse. He's breathing just fine, pulse is good and strong. He should wake up fairly soon, within an hour or so. Setting to work with the napkins, I use an old-fashioned Boy Scout's square knot on our house guest—*deck* guest. Square knots are best if you don't have a lot of rope to spare and a napkin is definitely not a lot of rope to spare. We don't have time to go looking for something longer.

This is a race.

Once his hands are tied to the bottom of the handrail that runs around the edge of the deck, I turn my attention to his feet. I've used up two napkins and have only one left. I open up the un-smashed patio door, exposing the big, thick centre beam where the two doors latch. Brian helps me pull the suited man around, and we bring his feet just past the beam and into the dining room. I tie his feet together on the far side of the beam, around his ankles. He is perfectly pinned to the deck. He can't move either hand, and they can't reach each other to untie the knots. He can't move his feet, either. They seem to have a house tied between them. I think the yellow napkins make a nice touch.

Quickly, I search his pockets for clues. They are completely empty. This guy is a professional. I suspect that if we had the time to walk up and down the street, we would eventually find his car with the keys still in the ignition. There is nothing more I can do with him, so I turn my attention away from him and towards the house.

It is almost completely black inside, especially the basement. The only light is coming from the streetlights that have now turned on. In the time since Dad dropped me off, the sun has completely disappeared. We make our way through the eerily silent house to my mother's office in the basement. It's a mess. Things are tipped over everywhere. I grab her laptop from off the floor and bundle up the cords, then grab a handful of alarm pens from out of their box and stuff them into my pocket.

Brian finds a set of miniature walkie-talkies, a receiver, and two sets of night-vision goggles. They're the same ones we "borrowed" for last year's class camping trip. They work great for sneaking up on people and making them scream—instant ninja.

My backpack was sitting beside the computer when I left for Brian's this afternoon. Now it lies empty and abandoned on the floor. I grab it and everything we've gathered gets piled inside. Brian takes what doesn't fit in mine and puts it in his. We head outside to wait for the pizza in the driveway, not bothering to close the front door.

I guessed right. Danny pulls into our driveway with a big smile and a small wave. We walk towards the car and hop into the back seat before he even gets the car in park.

"You boys must be hungry," he chuckles as he turns to hook his elbow over the seat and look at us.

"Danny," I ask, "What do you make in tips on a Tuesday night?"

"Not enough, little brother," he replies.

"How does forty bucks sound?"

"Fantastic." He squints at me. "What's the catch?

"Well, big brother," I say, "my friend and I need a lift to the airport. I'll give you sixty bucks for these pizzas and let you keep the change. I'll even let you eat one of these delicious pizzas while we are driving. All you have to do is take the long way back to the shop."

Danny eyes me for a second and then looks over at Brian who simply nods. "Why do you have to go to the airport?" he asks.

"I gotta meet my dad there." I reply. It is the truth after all. Danny eyes me for a few seconds. I can tell he's deciding. "Please?" I add. "I can't afford a cab and you haven't got anything better to do."

Danny shakes his head and laughs a little. "Show me the money," he says.

I hand him the cash, then open the pizza box and hand Danny a six-inch pizza as well. Danny takes the pizza with one last shake of his head and starts to back the car up out of the driveway.

I lean way back in my seat and call Dad. He answers as we start down our street.

"Go ahead," he says. "What have you got?"

"I've got a set of ear-buds and mini-microphones for Brian and me to keep in touch in case we get separated." I reach up and turn on the overhead light and look at the backs of the tiny walkie-talkie set. Once I have the numbers, I lean back deep into my seat again. "It says J5 on the back...so they transmit at 104.3. Tune into that on your radios, and if you guys are close enough you can listen in too. I won't be able to hear you, but you can hear us. Tell Jack."

"You have the transmitter frequencies memorized?" Dad asks in surprise.

"Come on, Dad. I'm Mom's favourite test subject. I know this stuff inside and out."

"I guess you do. Okay, what else have you got?"

"I've got one of the new receivers, a couple of alarm pens, a couple of infrared flashers, some night-vision goggles, and her laptop," I tell him as I make a quick inventory.

"Why do you have her laptop?" he asks. "You said she changed the password."

"Yeah, but she's only got about two dozen passwords. I didn't feel like guessing at it this afternoon," I confess. "I should have it cracked in a few minutes."

He's silent for a second. "We're going to have a talk about this later."

"Yup…" I've let the cat out of the bag. I really shouldn't have been so cranky about Mom changing her passwords again this morning. I wasn't really being fair to her. "Dad?" I ask.

"Yes."

"Tell Jack he needs to send three or four big guys over to our house to clean up a small mess on the back deck. The front door's open and the back door is…missing. They don't have to worry about tripping any of the alarms because the power has been cut to the house."

He's silent for a few seconds this time. "We're going to have a *long* talk about this later."

"Yup."

I can hear him clenching his teeth. I'm not sure if it's mad or scared.

"Dad?" I ask again.

"Yes?"

"We're fine, really, and we're heading to the airport to help you find Mom. Is she still there?"

"Her signal vanished inside the main terminal. She's still on the ground. They're organizing a search team but it needs to be plain clothes, not uniforms. I'm on my way there now. We should arrive in about ten minutes. I'll call you when we have her."

Not if I get her first, I think to myself.

We hang up.

"Danny," I say leaning into the front seat and using a bigger voice than I had been using with my dad on the phone. "I think we need a little change of plans."

"Yeah? What?" he asks, keeping his eyes on the road. The smell of pizza fills the air as I pass him mine, which I haven't had time to eat yet.

"I think we need to head to the Citadel, not the airport. It's a half hour closer, so I guess your tip just got bigger."

I lean over to Brian and speak in a quieter voice. "I don't think these guys are stupid enough to just take her to the airport and wait for us to come get her. Sure, the airport has lots of steel buildings where signals get messed up, but this has to be about the G8 summit."

"A diversion?" Brian asks in a rising voice. He glances over at me, his eyebrows raised like two combat caterpillars overtop of his eyes. "Yes! They sent the phone to the airport as a diversion! Oh, that's dirty!"

"What do you think? Should we go to the airport or the Citadel?" I ask.

"Citadel," he says with a firm nod of his head.

I nod too, and then open the laptop while he eats the last piece of pizza, and start trying to crack my mother's secret access code.

CHAPTER 5

It takes longer than I expected. Most people's passwords are easy to guess if you know a little bit about them. Seven out of ten people use either their own or a loved one's birthday, maybe even a wedding date. They pick a number that means something to them, so they can remember it.

I try our whole family's birthdays and come up with nothing. I spend ten minutes coming up with names: our names, the names of my parents' childhood pets, nicknames of people we know.

Sitting back against the seat as Brian peers over from beside me, I sigh in frustration. I whisper, "It has to be something simple. Mom's been stressed out for the past two months. She wouldn't have come up with something complicated to try to remember. She would have forgotten anything that wasn't right there in front of her."

"Okay, so what was in front of her?" he asks me. "What was on her mind the most?"

"Well, the summit, of course…and all the political leaders of the world coming here to Halifax…and her being responsible for their safety."

"Try something about that," Brian offers. He looks around the back seat of the car and then out the window for clues to the password. Outside the car is more interesting, especially now that we've entered the city limits. Danny is completely ignoring us, which is good. He's listening to the radio, has both hands on the wheel and both eyes ahead. I note with a smile that he drives *way* slower than my father.

I type in the names of the eight leaders who are headed our way tomorrow. No go. It doesn't unlock the computer. *Tomorrow*, I think. They are all arriving tomorrow and there's a calendar hanging on the wall just above the computer. I type in tomorrow's date.

Bingo.

The security page disappears, the main page opens up, and "You've Got Mail" pops up, front and centre.

"Yeah!" I yell, punching at the sky in victory, only to ram my knuckles into the roof of the car. It makes a dull thud and my middle knuckle pops.

The car swerves a little as Danny ducks his head away from the sudden sound. "Hey," he barks. "Take it easy back there or I'll stop here."

I feel sheepish as I glance over at my friend. His shoulders are scrunched up around his ears as if he's waiting for someone to clunk him over the head with a mallet.

"How about a little more dialling of the phone," Brian says as he relaxes his shoulders, "and a little less frightening of the driver. You almost made Danny drive off the road! Be careful with that war whoop of yours."

I ignore his sarcasm and dial the number. Dad answers on the first ring.

"I'm in, Dad."

"That's great news. They've set up a command centre in the executive lounge here at the airport. We should have her back any minute." Dad's voice is full of confidence, but something about it tells me he's not being all the way honest. "See you when you get here." I don't tell him we're taking a detour. We hang up, but I don't feel good about it.

"Anywhere here, Danny," I tell our pizza man. He navigates the car into a parking spot at the foot of Citadel Hill but doesn't turn off the engine. He leans back over the seat to look at us and asks, "How do you boys plan on getting back home?"

"No worries, big brother," Brian says. "Halifax has plenty of pizza joints." He chuckles, opens the door, and hops out. I follow his lead.

"Now what?" Brian asks to me as we watch our ride drive away.

"I'm not sure," I answer. We both look up at the tall, dark mound that is the Halifax Citadel at night. The only street lights are around the bottom of the hill. There are no lights on the steep grassy slope that leads up to the old fortress. It is a long, dark way to the top. "Might as well go for a walk," I suggest.

Brian nods and grabs my backpack. He reaches inside and hands me a pair of night-vision goggles, then finds another pair for him. They look a bit like fancy swimming goggles, except they're made from heavy black plastic and have black metal rings around each of the eyes, an on/off switch between the eyes, and a battery compartment beside the right temple.

"I'm not sure if we look like country kids lost in the city or scuba divers on a dry run," Brian says.

"I'm thinking trick-or-treaters who don't understand how the calendar works," I reply as we both pull the night-vision goggles on. They're already adjusted to fit our heads, seeing as we were probably the last people to use them. They squeeze our faces and make our upper lips curl out a bit. I've seen Brian wear them dozens of times, but he still looks funny.

Brian makes fishy kisses at me, then digs out two flashers and turns them both on. You can't see them flashing with regular vision. You can only see them through the special light filters built into the goggles. Even if you hide the flasher in your pocket, you can still see it flashing away.

They help the police tell the difference between the good guys and the bad guys in the dark. It's one thing to be able to see people running through the dark, but it's another thing to know which ones to apprehend and which ones you'll want to meet for coffee someday.

We slide the flashers into our pockets and climb out of the car.

The night-vision goggles have light detectors; they won't turn on unless the level of light drops below what normal human eyes can see. If the light level drops down too far, the goggles turn on and magnify what little bit of light there is. Much like a regular magnifying glass, except instead of making the picture bigger, it makes it brighter.

The older models were very dangerous. If a police officer was sneaking around in a house trying to catch someone, and using the old goggles to do it, all the criminal had to do was throw on the light switch. The old goggles would magnify that light and burn the user's eyes. The police officer would be blinded for a while after that.

The newer ones, like we have, work just like regular eyes do. They squint if it's too bright and open wide if it's too dark. If the change in light levels is too much, they blink and go black for a second or two, to reset themselves and save your eyes. Under the street lights, they aren't on at all. Brian and I head up onto the grass of the Citadel. The farther we walk away from the lights, the brighter and greener everything gets.

I look back towards Brian. The flasher in his pocket is blinking bright green. Looking down I can see mine is blinking pink. No one on the hill can see them but us. Well, no one without goggles.

We walk the entire way around the Citadel, moving up closer to the top at first. Through our goggles we can clearly see guards standing at the top of the wall that surrounds the old fort. They have a perfect view of their part of the hill and much of the city. To the south is a huge park called the Halifax Common. To the east and west is a mixture of shopping malls and apartment buildings. To the south sits the old town clock. It was built in 1803 and hasn't changed very much since. Beyond it lie the downtown core and the harbour. You can still see the water over the tops of the buildings.

Brian and I circle the hill, but neither of us sees anything, and I slowly grow more disappointed. I was sure she'd be here. Finally, we stop and look out at the harbour. The Old Town Clock is to our right so it isn't blocking our view.

"I don't know what I thought I'd find." I sit hard on the grass and, with a frustrated sigh, pull my goggles off.

"It's not time to give up, man," he tells me. "It's time to think." Brian eases onto the grass beside me and puts his hand on my shoulder.

I nod, but I'm frustrated.

"You didn't think she'd just be sitting here waiting for you to walk up and say, 'Hey guys, give me back my mother, please,' did you?"

"No," I answer, driving my hand through my hair.

"This is our first step, not our last. So come on, man, let's think. What's next? Where are we going to look next?"

I shrug.

"If they have your mom, it's because she's the one who controls all the electronics, and apparently they know that. So where do they need her the most? Where would she be the most use to them?"

"I don't know!" I snap at him.

"In Texas?" he says. "Would she do them any good in Texas?" He sears me with his sarcasm.

"NO! Of course she wouldn't!"

"Where, then?" he pushes.

"If they want her to do something to interfere with the electronics at the G8 meeting, she'll have to be within radio range."

"Good! Good," he says encouragingly. "So that means she's got to be close, right? If they're after something at the airport, then your dad and the rest of them are there and ready. If they are after something here at the Citadel, *where couldn't they be*?"

I don't answer right away, but I start to tingle. My brain is kicking into high gear. Get rid of the bad answers and all you have left are the good ones. "She can't be to the south of the Citadel," I start to say, "because that's just a big open field and the buildings at the other end are too far away to reach with any kind of radio signal."

"Right! Good! So that leaves that whole area out. The office towers would be hard to get your mom in and out of. They have cameras and security guards. I don't think they'd work either," Brian says.

"It would have to be someplace they could stay without being noticed," I agree. "Hotels don't notice who comes in and out so much, but the maids clean the rooms every day. That definitely leaves hotels out."

Then I feel it. The ground is moving. It starts low, like a hum, then builds to a vibration, and finally a rumble.

Brian presses his hands flat against the earth to better feel the vibrations. We look up and down the street to see if there's a transport truck thundering by. We can see the street, except where the Town Clock blocks our view. There's nothing. Almost no traffic at all, let alone any heavily loaded transport trucks.

Faster than it started, the rumbling stops.

"Well, that was weird," Brian mumbles.

"Yeah…weird," I answer, but we're both not really talking to one another. Our senses are focused on the vibrations coming from the ground and we're waiting to feel them again.

"Did your mom ever tell you anything about any spy gear that imitates earthquakes?"

"Nope," I reply, silently searching my head for answers.

"How about subways?" he asks distractedly. "Is there anything out there that feels like a subway but can track people above ground?"

"No," I say and roll my eyes. Brian watches too much television.

"Yes there is!" he insists. "I've seen it on TV. They use radio waves to shoot through the ground and when the radio waves bounce back, they can turn them into pictures and see what's in the ground. That's how they find towns and stuff in the desert. It was on National Geographic, man! *They* don't show stuff on TV unless it's real."

"Yes," I tell him. "They can do that in the desert because the ground is really dry and it's easy to see through sand. The pictures are created when the sound bounces off the rocks they used to build the walls with. The radio waves go through the sand and bounce back off the rocks. But *everything* under Halifax is rock.

"The signal wouldn't go anywhere. It would just bounce right back up, unless it found a hole to go down, like a well or something. Even then, it would just bounce around and come back out the hole...*out the hole*!" I yell, jumping to my feet. "Brian! You're a genius!"

Brian jerks back, hands still pressed flat to the ground, and turns to stare up at me. "I am?" he asks in surprise.

"Yes, you are!" I say, reaching out my hand to help pull him up.

"Why am I a genius, exactly? What did I say?" he asks hopefully, taking my hand and using it to haul himself to his feet.

"The signals, my TV-addicted friend. It's all about the signals! They don't want the signals to see *into the ground*, they want the signals to bounce *out of the holes* that are already there!"

"What holes?"

"The ones in the wall!" I say, starting to walk away.

"What wall?" he asks without following.

"The holes in the walls of the fort!" I call back.

"What are you talking about?" he yells, holding his ground.

"The Citadel was built with a double moat around it and a drawbridge between the two." I stop ten feet away and turn to face my friend in the dark. "Back in the old days, if anyone attacked the fort, they would have to climb those steep walls up there," I say, pointing at the dark building behind us. "At the top of the wall, they'd find a steep ditch, or moat, with another high wall on the far side. They'd have to go down into the ditch and up a second steep hill before they'd get to the actual fort."

"Yeah, so?" He takes two steps in my direction.

"Those two hills they have to climb over are actually hollow. They have tunnels in them that run in a complete circle around the fort. Built into the walls are thin windows that point into the ditch. They're gunner's windows. Once an attacker was inside the ditch, the people from the fort could safely run around from one side of the fort to the other and shoot out through the tunnels. The guy in the ditch would get shot at from the front and from behind, and he couldn't shoot back, because the shooters were inside those thick stone walls. You can run completely around the fort on two different indoor tracks and never go outside."

"Really?" he says looking up at the Citadel behind us with admiration and doubt in his eyes. "How do you know that?"

"My uncle Rob used to work at the fort when he was a teenager. He was there when the last G8 summit came to town. He said President Clinton put on shorts and ran both loops inside the walls and no one ever saw him." I back up a few steps and Brian slowly follows.

"How does that answer our question about the subway? You think they have a subway inside the walls?"

"No. I think they want to get inside those tunnels and send a signal *out* through the holes *towards* the fort. The tunnel's windows are all pointed at the fort."

"What signal do you think they want to send?"

"Well, actually, I think they want to *block* a signal. If you know the frequency of a signal, you can send a counter-frequency that will erase the first one. If the frequency of their communication system is seven, you can erase their signal by playing a frequency over top of it that runs at minus seven. Seven plus minus seven, equals zero…See what I mean?"

"Yes! If they can block their communications, the bad guys can do whatever they want, because the good guys can't talk to one another and won't know what's going on! They will be deaf and blind!"

"Exactly! They could plant bombs and kill all eight of the world's most powerful leaders without any of us being able to stop them."

"…So now what? How do *we* stop them? How are these guys getting inside the stone walls? Is there a door? The security guards must have the doors guarded."

"The doors are all well guarded. They're all inside the fortress. These guys can't get at the doors."

"So what good do the tunnels do them if they can't get at them?"

"I think they can get at them. They're just not using the doors to do it."

"Magic?" he asks, flapping his arms. "Are they just going to *abracadabra* themselves inside?"

"No," I scoff. "They're going in through the bomb tunnels."

"*What* bomb tunnels?" he yells in frustration, throwing his hands in the air and looking around us, stopping once again.

"Okay, listen to me," I say, grabbing his shoulders and making him look at me. I have to back up a little. I need to slow down and explain. "This old fort has two rings of tunnels that go all the way around the outside, right?"

"Yeah, I got that."

"There are five or six long tunnels that branch off the outside ring and run down the slope of the hill. The idea was that if the enemy started to come up the hill, the people inside the fort would be able to run down these ray tunnels and put explosives down at the end of them. Down near the bottom of the hill. Right?"

"Right…"

"The piles of explosives would be *behind enemy lines*. If they blew the tunnels up, it would take out lots of people and the enemy would have to retreat."

"Did it work?"

"Who knows? The Citadel has never been attacked. The French never got close enough to fire even a single bullet, let alone a cannon."

"So they have all these tunnels that run down the hill. So what? If these guys can't get in the front door, how are they going to get into the tunnels?"

"They're going to make their *own* door. They're digging their way in!"

"No way," Brian says. There's a long silence. "Someone must have noticed them digging. I mean, with all those security agents running around town, surely one of them would have noticed." He turns away from me and surveys the hill in the dark.

"Not if they started the tunnel from inside a different building. They could have started it in a basement somewhere. No one would ever see them working."

Again there's a long pause.

"No way," Brian says again. "The neighbours would notice all the noise."

"Not if you don't have any neighbours."

"We're in the middle of the city! Who doesn't have a neighbour?"

"The Town Clock," I say, pointing down the hill to the tall silent building in front of us. "The last person to live in the clock was a Halifax chief of police who moved out, like, sixty years ago. These security guards are used to big trucks going by and they probably wouldn't have noticed the rumbling sound."

"If these guys started out in the basement of the Town Clock, no one would hear them. Their tunnel into one of the fort's bomb tunnels wouldn't have to be big. Just big enough for someone to crawl through, while carrying a bunch of electronics."

"Where do you come up with this stuff?"

"The History Channel," I state.

"But *I'm* a TV addict for watching The Discovery Channel?"

"You didn't get that stuff about Egypt off the Discovery Channel. You got it off *The Magic School Bus*!"

"Who cares where I got it from?" He shakes me off, trying to change the subject. "Let's go have a look around the clock."

"I told Dad I'd tell him if we found anything. Shouldn't we phone first?"

He rolls his eyes. "We're not going to smash down the door and jump in there holding six-shooters or anything. We're just going to see if there's anything obvious. If everything is normal, there's no point in calling in the troops and looking like a couple of goofball kids. If we see anything that doesn't look right, *then* we'll call in the big guns."

"I guess you're right. Let's go."

This time when I start off, Brian is there beside me, matching my pace stride for stride. We have a purpose, but the closer we get the less hopeful I become. It really doesn't seem like there's anything going on around the clock. It's just dark inside. No light coming out of any of the windows. It's a silent, sleeping monument to the past.

We circle the building, running our hands over the rough cement and wooden surfaces.

There is no movement anywhere near the building. The lowest window that isn't covered by wooden shutters is about nine feet in the air.

"Let me get on your shoulders so I can look through the window," Brian says, tipping his chin up to get a better look at the high window. "I can use the wall to balance myself."

"You outweigh me by two elephants and a goat. There is no way I'm going to be on the bottom of this dog pile," I tell him. "I get the top."

He shrugs and drops his bag. "At least put on some goggles before you go up. You won't be able to see anything inside there without them."

It only takes me a few seconds to put the goggles back on. The familiar green glow starts up right away. I turn to see Brian. His hands are braced against the wall like a football player trying to push the building over. His feet are wide apart and both knees are bent slightly.

I put my first foot high up on his thigh, as close to his hip as possible, then reach across to grab his shoulder and start to pull myself up. He shifts a little under my weight. I reach the lip of the windowsill, take a second to find my grip, then pull myself up with both my arms and walk up my friend's back until I am in a crouched position on his shoulders.

"You good?" I ask.

"Mm," he grunts, but says no more. I can tell he's holding his breath and breathing sharp through his nose. He's working hard to hold me up.

"Is that *mm* as in yes, or *mm* as in no?" I ask.

"It's *mm* as in hurry up!" he says through clenched teeth. "I'm getting shorter by the second down here."

I smile at the thought, then straighten up and brace myself against the windowpane, cupping my hands on either side of my eyes to block any extra light from outside the building. My reflection is looking back at me. A head with night-vision goggles.

"Why would the Old Town Clock have mirrored windows on the bottom floor?" I wonder, then pass my hand over the glass of the window to try to wipe away any water condensation that might be making the glass reflective. But my mirror image doesn't move with me. Instead, it drops down out of sight on the other side.

It isn't my reflection, it's someone else looking out of the building! Someone wearing expensive night-vision goggles, and they're staring back at me. I jerk back away from the window in surprise, launching myself back with both hands. Beneath me, Brian tries to compensate and moves away from the building with me. We go too far. His shoulders shift and roll under my feet.

"What are you...?" Brian starts to yell.

I grab back onto the window ledge and duck below it at the same time, trying to get out of the view of the person inside. Again Brian's shoulders jerk wildly beneath my feet, this time back towards the building.

Ka-thunk I hear from below me, and know that Brian has been thrown into the wall. Given the sound of the impact, he must have hit quite hard.

Brian drops out from underneath my feet. My body swings forward and slams, belly first, into the building. The shock makes me lose my grip on the windowsill and I start to drop. Brian is somewhere below me and I don't want to land on him. Using one foot, I push myself away from the wall and to one side, hoping to avoid landing with my full weight on my friend's body.

The flash of the street light is enough to kick out the electronics and the goggles go completely black just as I turn in mid-air to fall to the ground. I can see nothing. I hit the ground faster than I expect, and my knees buckle from the impact. Pain jolts from my knees to my brain instantly. In the complete black behind the goggles, I can't even tell which way I'm falling so I can put my hands up to protect myself. Instead, I wrap both my arms around my head and try to scrunch into a ball.

I feel my left shoulder slam into the ground a fraction of a second before I roll forward and have my face smack into the building. Ripping the goggles off my face, I turn to find my friend. He's sitting on the grass, half facing the wall and half turned towards me.

"That wasn't exactly how I remember the dance moves from *Swan Lake*, but we must have been close," he says.

I take no notice of his sarcasm and snap my head around in both directions to see if anyone is coming around the corner of the building.

"Come on!" I say, scrambling to my feet and grabbing my bag and goggles from the ground. "We've got to get out of here!"

Brian doesn't argue. He knows I'm wouldn't joke about something like this. He pops up immediately, grabs his bag, and takes off beside me.

"What did you see?" Brian asks twenty seconds later as he catches up to me. I have no destination in mind. I'm just running, on the diagonal, up the hill and away from the clock.

"Goggles," I pant. "In the window, there was another pair of eyes. They didn't want me to know they were there either because they tried to duck out of sight."

"Do you think it was one of the G8 security staff?" he asks, grabbing at my arm to stop me and spin me towards him.

"No," I pant, looking over his shoulder in the direction of the tower. "They're *supposed* to be here on the hill, guarding stuff. They'd want to be seen. Only people who *aren't* supposed to be here would try to hide."

Brian looks back as well. "Do you think your mom is in there?" he asks quietly. He turns his head to look back up to the Citadel at the top of the hill. "We need to tell someone. There are plenty of guards up there. I'm sure we can get one of them to listen to us."

I hadn't thought of that. It makes my stomach roll over. Images of my mother locked inside that black and silent clock tower leap into my head. Fear and anger ripple down my spine in equal measures.

"Let's go!" I decide out loud. We both start running at the exact same time, like someone had fired a starter's pistol and only he and I could hear it. We reach the top of the hill in fewer than thirty strides.

"Hey!" I yell as we scramble up the steepest part of the hill. Without the goggles on, it's hard to see where the security guards are standing. "We need to talk to someone! We need some help!" Just as I climb the last step and start to straighten up at the top of the hill, Brian hooks my ankle with his and yanks it backwards. I flip forward and crash hard on my chest and hands.

"What are you doing?" I hiss back at him in shock and anger, as I try to kick away from him and roll over onto my back.

"Have you ever gone to the fair and played the duck-hunt game? Use your head, man! They might have let us run away, but if they're watching us, they're probably going to try to stop us from running to *tell these guys* we know where they're hiding. You and I running along the top of this wall will make a nice little game of duck-hunt for them."

My anger vanishes instantly. He's right. I'm not using my head.

"We need to get to the gate," Brian says. "These guys won't listen to us yelling at them from down here anyway." He grabs my shoulder and pulls me back down the steep bank of the wall. We run along its base until we come to the road that leads up to the main entrance.

There are ten-foot-tall stone pillars on either side of the heavy, black, iron gate that seals the fort at night.

It doesn't look guarded, but we both know better. Brian grabs the iron gate and gives it a shake.

"We need some help out here! We need to talk to someone!" I call with my cheeks pressed between the cold metal bars. No one answers.

I call again, and still nothing.

"We have news about Marion! I'm Marion's son. She's been here with you all week and now she's missing! I think I know where she is. Please! Come open the gate!"

Brian is yelling his own set of requests and arguments beside me, but I'm not listening to his. He could be calling out lottery numbers, for all I know.

"Can you think of any codes you could tell them?" Brian asks me loudly, still trying to shake the four-hundred-pound gate. "Is there something you could tell them that only she would know?"

"Petal!" I scream. "Code name *Petal!*" I remember from the office that they had given my mother a code name over the speakerphone. My voice rises with each word. "I have information on code name Petal. Now *open this stupid gate!*" I rattle the bars with all I've got, letting go my frustration.

A dark figure steps into view from behind one of the giant stone pillars. He is massive. My face looks squarely at his chest. He's wearing a suit and has both his hands behind his back. He looks quite relaxed. "You kids need to leave or we'll have to call the police," he says, calmly but firmly.

"Good!" Brian snaps at him before I can think of what to say next. "Tell them to bring a SWAT team with them. I think you're going to need the extra help."

"Listen, kid," he says with a small air of irritation. "This is a high-security area. We aren't going to put up with any pranks. You need to stop this and move—" he stops speaking in mid-sentence. He's listening to something, probably the thing in his ear.

Hope springs up in me like a geyser. Maybe someone inside has taken the time to look up what Brian and I have been yelling.

Magically, the big man in the suit comes alive again and starts moving closer to us. Whoever was speaking in his ear must have instructed him to get rid of us. "Step away from the gate," he orders in a commanding voice.

"No!" I scream, slamming my hand into the iron bars with everything I've got. It rattles slightly, but my hand stings far worse. "You have to listen to me!" The huge man steps forward but I refuse to back down.

He leans in close, inches from my own nose, and says very calmly, "The gates open outward. So unless you want to get hit when they swing open, I suggest that you step away from the gates, so we can let you in." I'm close enough to see his one eyebrow rise.

An electronic hum starts up on the other side of the gate. Brian and I release the bars and hurry back a few feet. Before we can think about heading into the fort, the huge man blocks our entrance by stepping out through the crack in the gate as it opens. He holds his hand up in front of him in a silent command for us to stop.

"I need to search you before you can come in," he tells us. Brain hurries to the wall beside the gate, braces his feet apart in a wide stance, and leans, spread eagle, against the wall with his hands above his head. The man watches him go but does not follow him. Instead, he turns to me.

"Tell your friend he watches too many cop shows," he says, pulling out what looks like a wide paddle. It's a metal detector, and he quickly scans me with it, checks my bag, pulling out the goggles, flipping them over then stuffing them back into the bag and returning it to me.

"Hey," he calls to Brian. "When you're done playing prison lockdown, how about you come over here and let me scan you."

Brian drops his arms sheepishly and comes over. Within a minute, the guard is finished and we're following him though the gates. They close behind us. Our feet crunch on the loose gravel as we hurry into the centre of the fort. We follow the huge man across the partially lit and completely empty courtyard and into one of the stone buildings that surround it.

Inside is bright. I have to blink a little as my eyes adjust. The room is all white and empty, except for the long wooden table in the middle of it and the six matching chairs that surround it. There is one man sitting at the table. He stands and walks towards us, extending his hand in front of him.

"I'm Dwight Horsnell. You must be Andrew," he says, extending his hand to me. We shake. His grip is firm but quick. "And that would make you Brian. Your family is in the Witness Protection Program," he adds turning to Brian and extending that same hand to him.

Brian nods in a surprised response. Brian's family being in the Witness Protection Program is supposed to be top secret. He turns to look at me, but I can only shrug. I have no idea how this man would know about that.

"So, what's up, boys?" Mr. Horsnell asks, catching our attention.

"We saw someone in the clock tower. A man wearing high-end night-vision gear," Brian tells him, still holding his hand. Mr. Horsnell looks down at his hand. Brian is holding it firm and not letting it go just yet. He wants this man's full attention. "If they aren't one of yours, then you need to go see who they are. We think they're planning on jamming your communications systems tomorrow."

"The old clock is out of range—" Mr. Horsnell starts to say.

"*Was* out of range," I interrupt. "They've dug their way into the original defensive tunnels under the fort. Whoever these guys are, they are planning to run right up underneath you, and you won't be able to see them." I'm not sure I have him, so I push on.

"Sir, I think they might be Russian. At the very least, they aren't English," I tell him.

"How do you know?" he squints his eyes at me. "You only say you saw him through the window. How could you hear him speak?"

"I didn't hear him speak, sir. But I heard one of his friends grunt about two hours ago at my house when he tried to shoot me."

"You're telling me a Russian hit man came after you and you got away?" he raises his eyebrows questioningly.

"He wasn't trying to kill me. It was a tazer. He was trying to catch me so he could use me as a weapon against my mother. If he was trying to kill me, he wouldn't have used a stun gun."

He thinks for a moment, then nods. "So how did you get away?" He asks.

"Well, I wouldn't have if it weren't for Brian here." I nod towards my friend. "Let's just say it was stew against one."

Mr. Horsnell stares at me. Brian finally releases his hand. He blinks twice, a sign that he's processing what we've said. "Take a seat, boys," he says, stepping back and ushering us towards the table with a sweep of his hand. "I'm all ears. What have you got?"

CHAPTER 6

In less than ten minutes, we've told them what we know—twice. First to Mr. Horsnell alone, and then a second time to three other men, whose names I instantly forget, and one female named Agent Smith, who has shown up as well. They all ask different questions:

"How do you know about the tunnels?"

"What makes you think they're digging their way in?"

"Could you tell which brand of goggles they were? Who was the maker?"

"Are you sure you only saw one person?"

Then suddenly they all stand up at once and start towards the only door. We stand up with them and fall in step once they pass us.

'Wait a minute, fellows," Mr. Horsnell says as he stops and turns at the door. "You two stay here and we'll have our people go check it out."

"No," I tell him flatly.

"Yes," he insists, pointing back at the table, as if we will go and sit in the corner like naughty puppies. "There is no way I can let you come with us."

"Then there is no way you'll catch them," Brian blurts out. "You don't know where the tripwires are, and we don't have time to tell you were every one of them is."

Before I have time to wrap my mouth around the words I'm thinking, Mr. Horsnell asks them for me.

"What trip wires?"

"The ones in the tunnels," Brian answers, straight-faced. "You won't find them on a map or blueprint, either, so don't bother looking."

"If we can't find them on the blueprints, then how do *you* know about them and where they are?" Agent Smith asks bitingly, her eyes sharp as daggers.

"His uncle Rob told us," he replies, pointing his thumb at me. "During the Second World War, they used these tunnels to train soldiers. Half the Second World War was fought underground, you know. The Germans were tunnelling like mad to try to get behind the Allied lines of defence. The Allies were going crazy trying to block the Germans' tunnels and still dig clever tunnels of their own. New troops got their tunnel training here on Citadel Hill. When the war ended, some of the tunnels were cleared out, but most were just left as they were. They didn't figure anyone else would ever need to go into them again."

"I don't have anything here about any army training happening in *any* tunnels," Agent Smith pipes up, shooting a look of disgust Brian's way.

"Not surprising, seeing as you didn't even know about the tunnels in the first place," he fires back. "Just let us come with you to the start of the tunnels and we'll tell you which ones have tripwires."

"Why can't you tell us from here?" she asks sharply.

"Because Uncle Rob didn't show us on a map, he just told us what to look for." Brian waggles his head like a little kid defying his mother over eating his green beans at supper.

"Then you tell us what to look for and we'll do it." She steps forward threateningly, but Brian matches her move by stepping forward too.

"If I could show you the picture in my head," he shouts, "then I would! But I can't generate Lexmark photos out of my forehead and Uncle Rob is out of town, so he can't help us either! Now are you going to take us into those tunnels or not?"

"Enough!" Mr. Horsnell interrupts, stepping between the two of them and waving his arms. "Agent

Smith, that's enough. They're here because Marion is his mother. What can it hurt to go check this out? It's highly unlikely, but if we just go look then we can at least eliminate it as a possibility." Turning to one of the men, he adds, "Get them some extra vests and helmets. They can come into the defensive hill, but not into the tunnels."

Brian has won. Agent Smith flashes an angry look then steps back and returns her expression to that of an annoyed librarian.

The entire group files out of the room, back through the courtyard. It is a far more active place than it was only minutes before. There are at least ten people standing in plain sight or hurrying in different directions. Two of those people emerge from a building, carrying boxes. They are running in a path to intercept us.

I look ahead in the direction we're headed and see a heavy steel-and-wood door. It has black iron cross-supports, and stands in the middle of the wall, just beside the main gate. There's a giant lock holding the door tight.

We pull up short in front of it and turn to watch the activity. A security guard hurries over with a huge ring of keys in his hands, searching for the right one. Two men carrying body armour arrive and start passing out vests and helmets.

He hands one of each to Brian and me. We watch the others pulling on their one-size-fits-all vests, and we figure out which Velcro spider-arm goes to which Velcro spider-patch. Magically the vests size down to fit two thirteen-year-old boys. The black helmets are a little too big, but the straps help hold them firmly to our heads.

The keys jingle in earnest, the lock clicks, and the door squeals open. This is the entrance to the inner tunnel, the one closest to the fort. We need to pass through here, go through the ditch of doom, and then find the door to the outer tunnel, where we really need to be. We follow along quietly.

As casually as most people take out an umbrella in the rain, Brian and I pull out our night-vision goggles and start to put them on.

Mr. Horsnell watches us, smiling. "We've got lights with us, boys, so you won't need those," he waves his hand at our heads. "You definitely are Marion's boys, aren't you? You're as at home with those goggles as I am." He chuckles a little and shakes his head, then leans closer to us and adds, "My kids think I sell insurance." He winks, then turns and enters the tunnel.

Mom's never lied to me about what she does. She's lied to everyone else on the planet, but not to Dad and not to me. This guy is the head of security for the biggest political meeting of the year and his kids think he sells insurance. Go figure.

We head into the dark tunnel single file. Ahead, someone turns on a huge light and the tunnel comes to life. The walls, floor, and ceiling are all made with smooth, dark rocks. It looks like an old wine cellar. The shadows created by the people in front of us dance and jerk along the walls as we move forward.

We stop. Keys jingle, and soon we are outside again, in the ditch. It takes a little while for us to get into the next tunnel. Apparently the locks on abandoned tunnels are not opened or oiled very often.

The second tunnel is identical to the first. It curves around to the left, a long, dark tube with stone walls and dancing shadows. Footsteps echo around us, making it sound like there are thirty people in the tunnels, not just seven.

"Witness Protection boy!" we hear Agent Smith's voice ring out ahead of us. "Come up here and tell us more about the picture in your head." There is a brief mumble of words from Mr. Horsnell. "Please," Smith adds, but it sounds like it hurts to say.

Brian and I move closer to the front. I have no idea where I am in relation to the objects above ground but assume we're now on the same side of the fort as the old clock. A dark shadow on the wall turns out to be the entrance to one of the offshoot tunnels.

Immediately, the grade in the floor tilts and matches the slope of the hill above us. The grade is steep, and the stone floor is black and damp and slippery. The huge light only goes so far down the tunnel before it fades and leaves us to wonder how far we have to go to get to the end.

I run my hand on the clean, smooth stones in the hope of balancing myself on the steep climb down. I'm watching my feet, not my hands, but it's my hands that first tip me off. I stop walking and look at my fingers, rubbing my thumb across the pads of each fingertip. They're gritty. There's a fine sand on the tips of my fingers.

"These walls are getting sandy," I call out, but no one pays attention. I think for a minute, but the light and other people are getting away from me. I start walking again, but my spider senses are turned up. I shift my feet over the stones. They aren't as smooth as they had been. My sneakers are detecting grit on the floor, too.

"Hey! The floor is getting gritty too," I call up ahead, but only Brian and Mr. Horsnell stop walking to turn and hear me.

"What do you mean, the floor is gritty?" Mr. Horsnell asks, looking down.

"All the other parts of the tunnel are clean. Now all of a sudden there's grit. How come?" I ask.

"We're getting closer to the roads. The vibration from the traffic could be making dirt sift out of the rocks and turning things gritty," he offers.

"We've had traffic for two hundred years. If it was that, the grit would be thicker than this. If they are tunnelling, they've only been doing it for a few days or maybe weeks. That would explain why the grit isn't thick."

"The closer we get to the source of the vibrations, the more grit should show up," Brian adds.

"Exactly," I confirm, but Mr. Horsnell still looks doubtful.

"Hold up!" he yells to the people walking away from us with our light source. We walk closer to where they are now standing still.

Again I swipe my hand on the wall. Gritty.

Mr. Horsnell swipes too. "The boys have a theory about vibrations causing dirt to filter out between the rocks," he says to the others. "Everyone keep an eye and a finger out. Let us know if you notice any sudden piles of dirt on the floor or anything that seems unusually dirty."

They start moving again.

"I think you might be onto something here. It's

worth sending someone out to look around the clock at least," he tells Brian and me. Then he takes out his communications piece, but I interrupt him.

"That won't work down here," I tell him. "The signal can't get out through all this rock." He nods and looks both ways up and down the tunnel. He's deciding. Again I interrupt. "How about I run up and tell them you want them to go into the clock?"

"They won't believe you all on your own," he tells me, shaking his head. "Larson!" he calls down the tunnel. "Take this young man back up the tunnel and tell them I give clearance to enter the clock. Turn the place inside out. Pay close attention to the basement." Then, turning to me, he asks, "Does it *have* a basement?"

I don't really know for sure, but I don't want to get left out because he thinks of me as a kid. "Yes, it does," I tell him. "My uncle Rob told me where the floor hatch is hidden and how to get it open."

He nods. "Larson," he says firmly. "This is a Code Red until somebody proves to me otherwise."

Larson nods seriously in return. Then he and I take off back up the steep slope of the tunnel. He's much faster than I am, so I drop my bag. Brian will surely see it when he comes back up the tunnel. He'll pick it up then.

Ten minutes later, two men have joined Larson and me, and we're standing at the front door to the clock tower. I look over my shoulder at the cars still driving by and the people walking down the street chatting happily as we start picking the locks and breaking into this historic monument.

"Give us a couple of minutes to sweep the place, then I'll come get you," Larson tells me as the door pops open and the first of them start to enter.

I nod, but have no intention of obeying. The second they clear the door I enter behind them. They creep along the walls, keeping their backs covered. I know there won't be anyone standing in the middle of the room just waiting to give up my mother. If she's here, she's either up in the tower or down in the basement.

I make a run for the stairs. I feel an arm sweep out to try to catch me, but jump to the side to avoid being grabbed. My adrenaline jumps into action as well, and with the added boost I dash for the metal spiral stairs in the middle of the room. They stretch up and down, with a small flat spot at this level. Grabbing the metal support, I swing onto the stairs and land on the third step down as I gain speed for my descent into the basement.

The stairs clang loudly and rattle as I throw myself down them. Someone swears behind me, and the sound of another set of feet just above me on the steps rings in my ears.

"Get down!" my pursuer yells at me from above.

I obey the second my foot hits the cement floor. The force of my landing jars my knees, and I allow them to buckle underneath me, turning my downward motion into a speeding side roll. With only the light coming in down the stairwell, the basement is almost completely black. I cradle my head with my hands and hope against hope not to hit anything too big or sharp.

Before I come to a full stop there are feet on either side of me and someone is apparently sitting on my hip. I start to fight him off automatically. A hand grabs my head and pins it to the floor.

"Stay still or I'll shoot you myself," Agent Larson hisses. From his perch on my hip he clicks on his flashlight. After a quick scan of the basement, which I follow intently from my spot beneath his weight, we find the basement is also empty.

"Clear!" he yells up the stairs. The others join us immediately. He yanks me up by the back of my shirt and I jerk out of his grasp, swatting at his hand. "That was just plain stupid," he tells me with anger in his voice.

"If they didn't shoot us the second we came in through the door, then they aren't here," I snap back. "We both know that. You're just following procedure.

My mother is missing and I don't care about your stupid procedures. So drop it, and start looking for clues about who these guys are."

He's quiet for a second. We both know I'm right— after all, we're both still standing here, with no new holes in us. We spread out and start searching the room for clues. I follow one of the guys with a flashlight.

"You told Horsnell about a hatch in the floor. Where is it?" Larson asks as he scans the floor with his beam of light.

"I lied about that so he'd let me come," I answer quickly. I'm busy dragging my foot across the floor. "The floor is gritty here too. Not just sand, either. There are little pebbles and small clumps of mud. They've been digging down here for sure. Look for wide cracks or scrape marks."

"Who *are* you?" one of the men asks in disbelief, pointing his flashlight at my face. It blinds me completely. I put my hand up to block the light. Before I can answer, the other man with us speaks.

"I might have something."

We all head over to his spot on the wall. It's a cinder-block wall. All the bricks are rough, light grey, and cemented together. The light glints differently off of one section of the wall, about three square feet. He taps it with the end of his flashlight.

It knocks like wood, not like cement. He turns to look at Larson. They find the edge with their fingers and work their way around. The side nearest me comes free, and the section swings open. It's been painted to look like the other walls.

The hidden door opens wide and we all crouch down to look inside. All three flashlights point through the opening at once and give perfect lighting to the earthen tunnel ahead of us.

We hold still for two or three seconds as we all process what we are looking at. Brian and I were right, but the tunnel looks deserted. Cans and boxes line the walls, but whoever was here has left. Probably after they saw me peeking in the windows.

Larson is the first to move. He crosses the threshold and is about to take the first step down into the tunnel.

Click.

We all freeze. It's a faint click, like a lamp being turned on, but it's a click. Empty tunnels don't click for no reason.

Larson's head is already inside the entrance to the tunnel. Slowly he turns it to the right. "It's an entrance alarm," he whispers. "Standard twelve-button pad. Can you disarm it?" he asks calmly over his shoulder.

"Not in the ninety seconds we've probably got," the man beside me answers.

"Then I guess we'd better run," Larson says as if he's ordering a hamburger. "Break!" he screams.

His scream and the eruption of movement from the people around me makes my heart jump into action. Surges of blood pump into my veins. My body turns electric, and we all move as one mass towards the stairs. Someone grabs my shirt and shoves me out in front of the pack. Our thundering feet echo around the basement walls, and it sounds like a million people are chasing me, urging me forward.

My legs take the steps two at a time. I'm flying, grabbing at the steps and the central pole to help pull me along with greater speed. We all know we have only seconds to clear the building.

"Go! Go! Go!" voices yell from behind me. I pray that I'm not slowing them down. My hair stands on end as my foot reaches the top step, and I sprint to the door.

Something has closed the door behind us after we all entered the clock tower. Maybe it was someone. The old wooden door opens inward, which will slow our progress in getting out of the building. In the five strides I have between the top of the stairs and the door, I try to figure out the fastest way to get the door open.

The question is answered for me as one hundred bullets spray the door from both sides of me. They have side-stepped me to allow more shooters at once. The roar of a hundred bullets a second is deafening. It sounds like it's coming from inside my head, threatening to burst out through my eye sockets and eardrums at the same time.

The door begins to shatter into a million falling, wooden pieces that spray up into the air and burst out in all directions. I throw my arm up over my face and continue pounding my feet in the direction of what I hope will be an opening by the time I get there. In seconds the door is free of its frame.

The bullets stop, half a breath before I reach the door. I can still hear them ringing in my head. A hand again grabs the back of my shirt and forces me through what is left of the shattered door. It may be mostly gone, but it feels very solid as my shoulder crashes into what is left of it. Pieces of wood rain down around my head as we smash through the opening, sending what's left of the door out ahead of us and into the night air.

The metal tube handrail on the other side of the entrance catches me in the hip, and the hand between my shoulders forces me over the rail, headfirst. My two hands reach out to grab anything to stop my fall. One hand gets a partial hold of the railing as I tip over it. It shifts my balance and throws my legs over my head like a cartwheel. My arm jerks taut, wrenching my shoulder, and my feet whip towards the ground at greater speed.

In mid-cartwheel, I can see more bodies coming out through the opening that was once a door.

A flash of light from behind the opening nearly blinds me. I squeeze my eyes tight and let go of the rail. I can hear nothing of the explosion that follows, but my whole body is sucked and squeezed as if by giant hands, as it falls towards the ground below the entrance landing.

My eyes pop open at the extreme pressure drawing the air out of my lungs. Looking up as I fall, I can see the last two people out of the building flying over me like circus trapeze people stretching their arms out to grab the swinging bar on the far side of the tent. But there is no bar.

Above the flying people is another burst of light. The explosion has reached the top of the tower. I watch in slow motion as the entire face of the clock explodes out of its brackets like a cherry pit being spat out of someone's mouth. I watch it as it stays vertical for a few feet, the face of the clock still intact, before it starts to spin and tumble.

Time flies when you're having fun.

Crunch.

My body finally catches up with my brain as I crash, full body, into the side of the tower and ricochet onto the grassy slope behind me. My chest feels like it has collapsed completely, but I ignore it and force myself to roll over and crawl closer to the foundation of the building.

Metal and wood fall around us like bombs, bouncing and sometimes exploding when they hit the ground. The clock face finally lands. It hits the sidewalk beside the main street at the bottom of the hill, where old fort turns into modern city. The face disintegrates into a shower of glass and metal. Red brake lights glow in both directions as drivers try to avoid hitting the falling debris and watch the clock tower disappear.

Two of the three people I was in the clock tower with are crunched tight to the wall beside me. The fourth, apparently knocked out by the impact, has not moved from where he landed in the grass. I quickly realize that he could be killed by debris falling off the tower.

Larson realizes it too, and we move away from the wall and towards the man at that exact second. We each grab a leg and haul him back over the grass and debris to the relative shelter of the cement wall. Larson immediately starts checking his breathing and pulse. It scares me to realize that the man I have just pulled across the lawn might be dead. My mind jumps to my own friend.

"*Brian*!" I scream.

Brian and the rest of the team are on the other side of that tunnel! When the tunnel blew on our side, it must have affected the old tunnel on the other side as well!

Keeping in a low crouch, with my shoulder pressed hard against the building, I start to move. I need to get to the other side of this building. The tunnel where I last saw my friend is on the opposite side of this building.

Fear for Brian overwhelms me, and I stop hugging the building and break into a full run. The debris is falling in smaller pieces now, and all around the base of the tower there are chunks of the building. Without looking up, I know it is completely destroyed.

When I come around the second corner of what was once a building, the light from the streets is blocked out again and it takes a second for my eyes to adjust. I blink them several times, even after they are focussed on the scene up the hill.

A third of the way up the hill, between the old clock tower and the Citadel, is a crater. A hole has opened up in the ground. Twenty feet wide by forty feet long. It looks like the dug-out basement of a very long house.

If my friend was in that tunnel when the explosion went off, he's now buried alive.

CHAPTER 7

Now that the explosion is mostly over, the people who gathered to watch it take two courses of action. Most, realizing that this isn't a free fireworks show, have started running away. I don't know whether they're screaming or not; my ears are roaring from the explosion. The rest of the observers are inching closer.

The security guards at the top of the walls are staying exactly where they are. They never leave their posts. I know that backup will soon be coming from every direction but I can't wait for them. My friend is buried alive and has to be rescued before he runs out of air.

Brian and the others only have a few minutes.

Jumping into the hole, I start pawing at the sod and grass. It, too, has been blown into chunks and pulls up in toaster-sized pieces from the ground. I throw the first one out of the hole.

"Help me dig!" I yell at the people who have started to gather around the hole. "There are people buried in here! Get down here!" I scream. "Get down here and help me!"

They do.

Men and women start carefully climbing and jumping down into the hole beside me and digging too. They respond to the urgency in my voice and dig fast. More people show up and pile into the hole. Some of the bigger chunks are taken out by two people at a time.

By the time the first secret service people arrive in full riot gear from inside the fort, we have made it down through the sod in some sections and are digging at stones. There couldn't have been more than two or three feet of earth over top of the tunnels.

Some of my hearing is starting to come back. The roaring has turned to ringing and I can make out voices and tones above it, but not words. Everyone is talking and yelling and digging at the same time. In the distance I can hear sirens. Police, fire, ambulance, I can't tell. It's probably all three.

Fear has given me muscles I didn't know I had. Huge rocks feel like nothing as I dig and throw as fast as I can. I'm panting hard, breathing in chunks of air and blowing great huffs.

The crowd around me shifts and hurries off to one point. I lift my head in their direction. They've found something! Scrambling over the rubble I see the arm sticking up out of the rocks. I pitch in. Some people are pulling on the arm and others are just digging like mad. The arm is in a suit. It's not Brian, but I dig furiously along with the others.

The man who gave me the bullet-proof vest earlier is pulled from the debris. A paramedic appears as if out of nowhere and checks his pulse. Two seconds later, the paramedic nods his head and gives the thumbs-up sign to the crowd around him. My heart surges in my chest. Hope. Hope that it's not too late for my friend.

The injured man is rolled onto a stretcher and carefully lifted up out of the hole. The crew is growing as more people file in to try to help dig. Spurred on by the success of finding one man alive, the group digs even harder. Spotlights and car lights begin to illuminate the area, making digging easier and faster.

A second and third person are found. Each one gets the thumbs up and loud cheers, as they clear the hole. One of them comes out of the debris moving his arms and legs a little as he tries to help. The other is a complete rag doll. My panic is starting to build. There is still no sign of Brian.

Think! I scream at myself. *Where would he be*? I turn away from the group and head closer to the Citadel, farther from the clock tower. They would have kept Brian farther back. If they were still in the tunnel, it must have been because they found something too. They wouldn't have let Brian get close. He was probably partway up the tunnel when it blew.

"Over here!" I yell. Several people join me. We dig relentlessly for four or five minutes. It's getting urgent. The brain can't go more than a few minutes without oxygen.

Someone lets out a war cry that even I can hear, and I turn to see them pull a backpack out of the dirt. It's Brian's. I scramble over and grab the bag out of his hands. Ripping it open, I start screaming, "Kill the lights! Kill the lights!" but no one understands.

Pulling the goggles out of the bag, I shake them at the secret service agent standing nearby. "Brian has a flasher! I can find him with these if you kill those stupid lights!"

He turns from the top of the crater, and waving his arms wildly he adds his voice to mine. Shouts of "Turn off the lights!" ripple over the crowd in waves. Most of them don't understand why I want the lights out, but they yell the command anyway.

The lights click out in clusters as people run to obey the newest command, and darkness returns in a rolling wave of shadows and blackness.

I pull on the goggles and flick the switch. The strange green glow appears. It's extra dark down in the hole. The light from my own flasher blinks up at me from my own pocket.

Then, near the edge of the hole, I see a pale flash squeeze out from around a shape in the dirt. The light is making its way around a rock and is barely visible.

"*Over here!*" I scream at the top of my lungs, lunging forward to where the faint glow popped up and disappeared again.

Somewhere a light comes back on and in an instant the goggles cut out and blind me. I pull them off and throw them, diving in with both hands. I drop to my knees to dig faster. Brian must have been leaning against the wall.

Rolling away a rock, I find a pant leg and start yelling my friend's name. My voice is high-pitched and panicky.

The rest of the crew swarms to the spot and parts of my friend's body emerges from the dirt. He is curled up in a ball with his hands over his head, protecting himself. He must have had at least a fraction of a second's warning before the ceiling came down.

Fear churns in my guts like acid. I don't wait for the next available paramedic. As gently and quickly as possible I bat the dirt away from his face, yelling at him the whole time. I clear more dirt from around his neck and shove my fingers just below his jaw, searching, but I can't feel anything other than my own screaming pulse exploding through my fingertips.

I grab him with both hands and shake him. The paramedics arrive beside me. They try to pry me off of him, but I won't let go.

"Open your eyes!" I scream, trying not to burst into tears. "Open your eyes!" They pull me more forcefully. It's their job. They need to work on him. They need to see if he's still alive. They need to make him breathe again if he has stopped. They need to save his life.

I let go, resolved but afraid. I need to let them take over. Brian drops back into the dent in the ground that I have lifted him from.

Then he moans.

I can hear it. Brian moans and my heart leaps into my throat. Tears squeeze out of my eyes, but I don't move. I melt into the ground and let the tears slide down my face. My entire body has given itself over to uncontrollable shaking.

The paramedics do their job. I sit, shake, and watch. By the time they have him on a stretcher and are lifting him out of the hole, he has started moving his hands. He's still moaning.

Once the extreme emergency of getting Brian out of the hole is finished, someone comes to lend me a hand. Grabbing the bag at my feet and the goggles beside it, I allow them to help. I find strength in my wobbly legs and follow the stretcher out of the hole, past the ring of fire trucks and police cars. Lights are flashing all around me, sirens wailing as new vehicles approach. People are pouring in from the nearby streets and buildings. All coming to either help or see. There's yelling in every direction as police, fire fighters, and regular people try to mobilize into action and help. I ignore them all.

With a paramedic at each end of the stretcher, a free space opens up beside my friend. I break away from my own helpers and jump ahead to jog along beside Brian, taking his hand from his waist where they have placed it. I squeeze it and call his name again.

Brian coughs and flutters open his eyes. I get in close so he can see me. His eyes come into focus and he blinks hard. I jog beside him all the way to the waiting ambulance, only letting go of his hand as they lift him into the back. One man heads forward and climbs into the driver's seat. The second man steps out the back to shut the doors. I step past him and start to climb in the back of the ambulance to be with my friend. He stops me at the door.

"Sorry, son," the man says calmly with a voice full of authority and assurance. "We can't let you ride along unless…" Suddenly he grabs my shoulder and tips me into the light pouring out of the back of the ambulance. "Cripes! What happened to you?" he stammers as he leans forward to look at my chest. "Are you all right? Here, sit down!" He tries to push my bum towards the bumper to sit me down.

I follow his intense glare and look down at my own chest. In the light spilling out of the back of the ambulance I can see the front of my shirt is dirty— but more surprisingly, there are ten or fifteen wooden splinters standing straight up out of my shirt. It looks like I've been attacked by a porcupine with wooden quills. The black square that covers my chest confuses me for a split second before I realize that it's not my shirt. I'm still wearing the bullet-proof vest!

I look past the man examining my chest and back up towards the clock tower. The dome at the top is now completely gone. The entire tower that housed the clock face is gone. My mind flashes back to seeing the clock face fly overtop of me and land by the street below. The house-like structure upon which the tower sat is mostly missing as well, with just a few partial walls left. Only the concrete foundation remains mostly intact. The ground around it is littered with pieces of the building.

I look back down at myself, mystified.

"I was in that building when it blew," I say, half to myself and half to the paramedic who is now looking at the pieces of wood sticking out of me, fingering them gently. There are a few bloody spots on my arms and shoulders. I suddenly realize they hurt.

"You might want to check my back, too," I say, turning around so the light from the ambulance can shine on the other half of me. "I seem to recall getting most of the blast back there."

"Most of the blast?" he asks in astonishment. "Son, you'd better come with us and let the doctors have a look at you." He changes the stern and authoritative voice to that of a concerned and helpful mom as he uses my elbow to help lift me into the ambulance. Two minutes ago I was okay enough to run around in the dark and hurl boulders, now I'm an old woman who needs help crossing the street.

I take a seat up by my friend's head. The doors at the back slam shut and within a few moments the ambulance starts to roll off the grass, over the curb, and down the street towards the hospital. The sirens are wailing and lights are flashing. It seems impossible that only two hours ago we were watching our favourite pizza delivery guy drive away from this very spot.

In the relative quiet of the back of the ambulance, Brian smiles up at me and points at my shoulder. "That'll leave a mark," he says.

I look down at the two-inch piece of wood sticking out of my shoulder. I reach up and pull it out. The small dot of blood that once marked its spot becomes a slightly bigger dot of blood, but it isn't a deep wound. I'm sure it will be fine.

"Girls love scars," I answer, shrugging my shoulders. "I should rub some charcoal into it to make it look really good. Imagine the stories I can tell them on the beach with that one."

Brian chuckles, then winces from pain and grabs his chest. "Well, you won't be able to tell them the real story, will you, because no one will believe you. You'll have to make up something more believable, like alien abduction or time travel."

We both laugh. We're okay.

Chapter 8

"What happened down there?" I ask after a few seconds of silence.

"Well," he begins after clearing his throat, "after you left, we started finding more gritty spots. They turned into little piles of sand and mud. By the time we reached the end of the tunnel, there were entire rocks that had fallen out of the wall.

"They started tapping the wall to see if they could tell where the new tunnel was going to come through, then all of a sudden someone yells 'run!' So we do, man!"

They must have heard the click too. Brian continues. "Everyone just starts running up the tunnel. I wasn't allowed near the end, but I still saw the wall go! It blew up, man! A rock hit me here." He points to his bottom rib. "It knocked me flat on my butt. I tried to get to my feet and scramble backwards. The tunnel walls held for a second and I thought it was over, but then the stupid roof fell in. I barely had time to duck."

"Are you good now?" I ask, worried and guilty and relieved at the same time. In a way, I caused the explosion and the tunnel collapse.

"Yeah, I think so," he says then looks around a bit, thinking. "Yup, I'm good... You? What happened to you? Did you find your mom?"

I shake my head and tell him what happened in the clock tower and then what happened after. We sit silently for a few moments as the ambulance races down the road, sirens wailing.

"You going to tell your dad what happened?" Brian asks.

"Not today, I'm not," I say emphatically, shaking my head. "If Dad finds out, he'll try to make me sit this one out, and I'm not going to let that happen. I'm in this until we get my mom back."

"Not telling him might be hard to avoid. When we get to the hospital, they're going to try to notify our parents. I think it's the second question on the medical form. It goes, 'Name' and 'Who do we call?' in that order, closely followed by 'What's wrong with you?'" He's still funny. Even wounded and strapped to a stretcher.

The ambulance slows, then stops. Within moments, they open the back door. Brian is unloaded, still on his stretcher, and I climb out under my own power.

The driver is there to lend me an elbow. The nurse who greets us at the emergency room door shows us through a sea of stretchers and running medical staff to a private room down the hall. We are not the first to arrive. It's like a three-ring circus except the clowns are all wearing scrubs.

Brian is unstrapped and transferred to a hospital bed where he's instructed not to sit up. I take a seat beside him in a chair. The nurse makes us take off our bullet-proof vests and gives us a quick once-over, but there's nothing major that she can see. She says that there is a waiting room full of people on top of the three that came in ahead of us and the doctor is dealing with the most serious cases first. The admissions clerk will be along soon to take all our information. She pulls the curtain around us and disappears.

"So, how do we get out of here?" Brain asks me the second the curtain stops moving, as he swings his legs off the bed and stands up. "I'm thinking we still have a mom to find and a world to save."

I bend over and peek under the curtain. "Do you want to head straight for the back door or should we fake a trip to the bathroom first?" I ask.

"Bathroom," he answers, "if I look half as dirty as you."

I look up at him, confused. He's smiling. I look down at my hands. They are completely black with dirt. In the bright hospital light I can see how filthy my shirt sleeves are. The bullet-proof vests and Brian's bag are sitting by my chair. The vests are dusty but other than that still whole and new looking. Apparently they're dirt-proof as well.

Grabbing our vests, we slip out from behind the curtain and stride with purpose to the public bathroom. If you walk like you know where you're going, people very rarely interfere.

We find the men's room. It's my first chance to look in the mirror. My shirt has bloody spots on it, and my face is full of smudges. I must have wiped the sweat off my forehead several times while we were digging. We look at each other in the mirror. I might be dirty from digging, but I'm not as dirty as my friend who was buried.

Using hand soap, water, and the scratchy brown paper towel, we clean up as well and as quickly as we can. The nurse might notice we're missing any minute. Our skin and hair are easy to clean, but our clothes are a mess. It can't be helped.

Using the same purposeful walk, Brian and I head for the front door. We don't look left or right, we simply stride forwards with our eyes facing front as we walk past the nurse's station. They don't raise their heads or bat an eye. They are too busy to notice us. We sail past.

As we reach the front doors, Brian asks, "Where to now, chief?"

"We need to get to the airport. There's no way this is over. You don't make a plan that big without backup. We just have to figure out what it is."

"How do we get to the airport? Can we order a pizza and have it delivered to the hospital? I've only got a couple bucks. Enough for a can of pop and two garlic fingers," he says as we step out the front doors of the hospital.

In the looped driveway in front of the main doors of the hospital are five news vans. Immediately, five reporters shove fuzzy microphones into our faces and start yelling questions at us faster than we can answer them. Five camera operators stand behind them with their glaringly bright lights blinding us.

"We just deliver pizza!" Brian yells at them. Immediately, the microphones drop and the lights go out. We walk away, hugging our bullet-proof vests, hoping none of the reporters are smart enough to know what they are, or to notice that we're way too young to be pizza boys. We walk quickly away and head down the driveway, alongside all the news vans. Brian and I both stop.

"They have cars," I say.

"They have *five* cars," he corrects. "We only want one."

"Yes," I say. "And only one news crew has 1-800-FOR-TIPS written on its side panel." I pull the cellphone from my pocket and punch in the numbers. We watch as one of the reporters starts digging into her purse. She grabs a phone from her bag, flips it open, and buries it under a giant mop of puffy blonde hair. Presumably putting it to an ear she has hidden under there.

I hear her voice, irritated, say "Krista Armstrong here."

"If you want the best story of your career, you need to get into your van and drive it out of the parking lot right now. Turn left as soon as you're out of sight of the four other news vans beside you, and stop."

"Who is this?" she asks, tucking her chin down to block the sound of her voice from the others. "Where are you? Can you see our van?" She turns away from the others and walks toward the TV station's van. The camera operator notices and follows her. "Were you part of the explosions on the hill?"

"Yes, we were at the hill. It was only one explosion, and we'll tell you all about it, but we're going to have to make a trade. Okay?" I ask hopefully.

"What kind of trade?" she asks suspiciously.

"You'll have to drive around the corner to find out. Just drive out of the parking lot and stop on the side of the road once you're out of eyesight of the others. Now, or the deal is off," I say in a stern voice, and hang up.

"That was pretty harsh!" Brian says. "What if she doesn't come?"

"She's a reporter. They're all snoopy," I answer with a shrug. I don't even look back to see if she's moving towards the van. I just start walking towards the pickup spot. "They'll go anywhere to get a story."

In no time, the van is stopped beside us on the side of the road. Brian and I open the back and climb in quickly, slamming the door shut behind us.

"I remember you," says Krista, in tall, black spiky boots, a long, dark coat, and hair like a deep-fried cotton ball. She squints at us accusingly. "You said you were delivering pizza."

"Who orders pizza at a hospital?" Brian asks her, with a tilt of his head. Then he holds up his vest. "This isn't a pizza-delivery box. It's the bullet-proof vest the police gave me to wear before things started going bad downtown."

He gives her a moment to look at the swinging piece of clothing. "We have a story to tell and if you want to hear it, you'll have to do a little driving as a trade. Deal?" he asks.

"Where? Where do we have to drive? What's going on?" There's excitement and doubt in her voice at the same time.

"Airport," I answer firmly. "And I'll talk to you as soon as I make this call." I pull Brian's phone out of his bag and start to dial.

"Agreed," she says. "Now get in the van before anyone else sees you. Barry, pack up the gear and let's go," she barks at the camera operator.. The van begins to roll and our new friends Krista and Barry speak quickly in hushed tones.

As we drive past the Citadel, it's in complete chaos.

There are hundreds of people there, standing three and four people thick in places. This kind of chaos in sleepy Halifax is big news. The police are trying to push them back, and they've got bright yellow police tape. Police cars line the streets, blocking the sidewalks and even some of the grass. Fire trucks wait just in case something bursts into flames.

My call connects.

"Please tell me you didn't have anything to do with the Citadel," my father says immediately.

"How could we? We're just driving past, and we can't even get close," I tell him innocently. It's not exactly a lie. "There are police lines everywhere. Did you find Mom?"

"No, we haven't found her yet. The Citadel is now officially out as the site for the G8. They're scrambling to reroute everyone. I'm sure they have a backup plan. Speaking of plan, we could use you here."

"I'm on my way, Dad," I say. "I just wanted to let you know. We'll be about forty minutes."

I hang up before he can ask me what's taking us so long. We should have been at the airport ages ago. He's been so worried about Mom he hasn't checked in with me yet, but he's not going to be happy about how long my trip to the airport has been.

Krista sees me hang up and climbs through from the front seat to the back with us.

"I've held up my end of the bargain. Now you hold up yours," she says, leaning in close and scowling. I think she's trying to sound tough. "Start talking," she says, shoving her recorder under my nose. "And it had better be good."

Chapter 9

Krista agrees not to use our names or our faces. We can't tell her the truth. The last thing I can do is tell her that my mother is a real-live spy-gear salesperson and that the company that makes it is right under her nose. I can't exactly give her the address to our house and send her there to find the would-be killer stretched out on my back deck with a house tied between his legs. Still, we have to tell her *something*.

I'm a great liar, but my mind goes blank. Brian saves me.

"So my friend here has an uncle." He points his thumb at me and Krista moves the microphone over towards him and out from under my nose. "Uncle Rob works at the Citadel and he got us inside for a tour. While we're in there, they get a tip about something going on in the clock tower. We don't know who they are, but they aren't locals. So the guys inside make everyone put on bullet-proof vests and they go to investigate it.

"We aren't supposed to be there in the first place, so they kick us out and tell us to get as far away as possible and to turn the vests in to any police station we like. We were just getting to the road below the clock when the bomb went off." He points at his shirt. "Which is why are so dirty."

He tells her in great long detail about how the clock tower exploded, sending wood and debris in every direction, and about the huge crater that was left behind when the tunnel collapsed.

I listen to my friend in amazement. He wasn't even in the clock tower, he's just taken what I told him and turned it into a really exciting story. I add the part about the face of the clock flying out and smashing on the sidewalk. And I managed to use my line about time flying when you're having fun.

Krista gobbles it up. It's a long ride to the airport. We have to create a story that lasts forty minutes. Brian's on a roll. I assume he has a plan, so mostly I just listen to him and nod when it seems like he wants a little backup. He mixes enough true things in with it that he's even starting to convince me.

"We weren't sure what to do then," Brian continues, "so we just hung around for a bit. And that's when we saw them."

"Saw *who*?" she asks eagerly, shoving her recorder even closer to his nose.

"Three guys running. They looked suspicious because they were all running away from the tower while everyone else was running towards it. To help, you know?"

"Yes! AND?" she questions excitedly, nearly salivating.

"And," he says, raising his voice. "And this van pulls up almost right beside us and these guys practically knock us over as they hurry to get into it. As the last guy was jumping into the van I heard someone with a Russian accent say something about the airport. So that's why we have to hurry and get there so we can warn them these guys are on their way."

"Why don't you just call the police and leave a tip?" she asks. I get the feeling she's almost forgotten to be a reporter, she's so caught up in Brian's story.

"Because I'm thirteen," he says with a roll of his eyes. "My voice still cracks. There's way too much going on tonight for the cops to listen to a squeaky-voiced thirteen-year-old. Besides, I don't think I could describe the men, but I could probably point them out in a crowd."

Krista's hanging on to his every word. We pull up outside the departures door.

"Thanks for the ride," I say, pulling open the side door.

"Thanks for the story!" she tells us.

I feel a little guilty for lying to her so much, so as a gift I add, "Don't run away too soon. There might be a second story here tonight. You should hang out here for a while."

She smiles at me like she's been crowned prom queen and hands me her business card.

We leave her in the news van and enter the airport. I know just where to go. It's where we always go when we're in an airport with Mom—the Air Canada Executive Lounge.

Airports have waiting areas with rows and rows of hard plastic seats that are easy to wipe down and clean up. Boring, empty spaces full of uncomfortable chairs, pop machines, and magazine stands.

Bigger airports have special rooms full of soft couches, big armchairs, widescreen TVs, and free snacks. These cozy little executive lounges are for people who travel often and have enough money to pay to get into them. They're nice.

We head straight for the Air Canada lounge on the main floor of Halifax's Stanfield International Airport. The airport should be almost empty this late at night, but there are soldiers, police, and airport security staff everywhere. They ignore us completely as we pass.

The lounge is not its usual quiet, cozy self. It's like a command centre from a Hollywood movie. The room is packed with people in business suits, security guards, and police officers, all clustered in pockets. Everyone's speaking at once. Again, no one notices us—we're just kids. I see Jack and my father at the other side of the room and we make our way over.

"Dad? Jack? Did you find her?" I ask with a surge of hope.

"Not yet," Jack answers. "We're trying to do a search without panicking the passengers. Her signal is still coming from inside the airport, but there's so much metal it's acting like a hall of mirrors and the signal keeps bouncing around."

Dad turns in his chair and looks at us for a moment, then hangs his head. I think he is silently counting to ten. Brian and I cleaned up as best we could at the hospital, but as I look down at our clothes I admit we might need to do some explaining.

"We have our first incoming VIP," someone calls out from the room behind me.

"Which VIP are we starting this show with?" Jack asks over my shoulder.

"Russian president," the same voice answers.

"Why are they keeping her?" I interrupt. "They've already had their plans ruined. The G8 summit will have to be moved. There's no point in keeping her."

Dad finally quits his counting and comes over to inspect Brian and I. It feels like a police pat down. Brian accepts it, but I fight back. I don't want to be treated like a kid. Not now. Not today.

"Son," Jack says, "We don't know if that's why they took her in the first place. We have to assume they have other plans and need to keep her for those. If we can figure out what their overall plan is, we can wreck it. Until then, we focus on getting your mother back and let the G8 worry about the G8."

Dad finally seems satisfied and gives my shoulder a quick squeeze and a nod, and then heads back to one of the computers. It makes me feel a little better. Brian has gone for a snack; he's at the muffin counter. Standing in the middle of the crowded room, I open Mom's laptop. Perhaps there's a clue there.

The second I open the lid, *ping*—an email notification pops up again. I open the inbox. What could it hurt?

"I think I've got something," I tell the entire room. A tingle runs up my spine.

"What?" Jack asks, stepping towards me.

"Mom tried to text us from her car while she was

being forced off the road. Look at the time stamp on this email. She must have written it on her way into the field." I feel a surge of pride in my mom. "She didn't want the phone beside her head, so she texted us instead. That's why she drove so far into the field. She kept driving through the ryegrass to give herself more time to type. I think she sent it to her laptop so we'd be able to start tracking her with all the software on here if we weren't already."

"What does it say?" Jack asks, peeking over my shoulder at the screen.

"Here," I say, pointing at the message. "Blk lnkn tn cr frm plt."

"What the devil does *that* mean?" Jack asks in a raised and frustrated voice.

"It's shorthand," I tell him. "It says 'black Lincoln Town Car with farm plates.' You just say the consonants and the vowels fill themselves in mostly…"

Jack raises his eyebrows and looks from the screen to me to my father. "They don't put farm license plates on Town Cars." Turning to the man sitting on the couch in the corner he barks, "Call the Department of Motor Vehicles. Find out which farmer is now missing the license plate off his tractor. It might give us a clue about where these guys came from, which might tell us where they're going."

The man on the couch looks up. It's Devon from the office. He says nothing, but nods and attacks the keyboard of his computer.

"Shouldn't we start by looking in the parking lot?" Brian asks in a louder-than-normal voice. Everyone turns to look at him. His mouth is full of muffin. He shoves it into one bulging cheek and continues, "Umm, I don't mean to interrupt, but if you know what vehicle she drove off in, and you think she's still here, shouldn't the Lincoln with the farm plates still be in the parking lot?"

After a few murmurs and a few quick glances, heads start to nod.

"Call the parking enforcement people out there. Tell them to start looking for this car," Jack says to one of the airport security people. They nod and half the room disappears at a dead run. The rest of the room is a blur of phone calls and barking orders as they mobilize to check the parking lot.

"How far out is that Russian flight and which runway are they coming in on?" Jack asks into the room after a few minutes.

"Russia's presidential plane should be touching down in fifteen minutes," a tall man answers. "They're landing on the emergency runway, right in front of the main building. They'll be landing so close to this building we'll be able to wave at the pilot as he's landing. They don't want any fender benders between this plane and any other planes in the parking lot. The pilot basically lands, and parks, all at the same time."

"I got something," Devon calls out. All heads turn his way. "We're clear! We're clear! I've got two signals. That's good enough for me," he says, standing up and grabbing his coat off his chair. "She's on the parking lot side of the building. I think they're moving her!" He heads for the door without looking back to see if anyone is coming with him.

Walkie-talkies and cellphones come to life as the room empties all the way. Everyone is on the move, including me. A hand hammers onto my shoulder.

"Stay back," my father orders. He pulls me behind him and heads out the door.

Brian and I follow but stay out of the crush of feet running through the mostly empty hallways towards the exits. Soldiers and police fall in. By the time they reach the exit, there are about twenty people who emerge from the building.

Police cars pull up and officers pile in. Black cars filled with people in suits come to a screeching halt at the door and more people in suits pile in. Dad hops into the same car as Jack and they screech away, leaving Brian and me standing on the curb, staring after them.

I'm furious at being left behind. My blood boils and I could scream.

"Boys!" I hear, but don't pay attention. "Boys, what's going on? Can you give us a statement?" I turn to see Krista. She has more red lipstick on than any one woman should ever be allowed to wear in a week, let alone all at the same time.

"They're chasing a black Lincoln Town Car with stolen farm plates," I hiss. I know I shouldn't tell her anything, but I'm so angry I can't help it. "They could really use the public's help finding it. Can you get that on the air as an emergency bulletin?" I ask. I have to *do something*!

"Are you serious?" Her jaw drops. Even her microphone drops a few inches.

"Yes," Brian interrupts me, cutting me off before I say too much. "I think the public needs to be warned. Tell people not to approach the car themselves, just call the police if they see it. The car has radioactive materials in it and it's really dangerous. These are environmental protesters from Russia! The Russian president is flying in at any second. You never know what they'll do next." He says it all with a straight face.

I've never heard anything so silly in my whole life. I have to take a second to marvel at it.

"I'm on it!" Krista announces. She's super-keen. "Thanks for the tip." She starts to head back to the van.

"That's an anonymous tip!" Brian calls. She gives him a thumbs up as she runs back to the van.

"Don't go anywhere." He calls after her again. "It could be a really busy night. We might have more stuff for you later."

Her eyes go wide. We head back inside. There's nothing more we can do from out here.

Inside, the regular people who are left are all looking around trying to figure out what's going on. Some are standing beside their seats; others are just craning their heads. Above their heads is the screen that displays the arrivals and departures of all the flights. The first five flights on both boards are yellow—all those flights delayed, just so they can land the Russian president without any traffic on the runway.

"The runway..." My feet stop moving and I stare at the board.

"The Russian president landing at any minute... Brian," I say slowly as I put the pieces together.

"What?" he says, looking around.

"They're using Mom's phone as a decoy. They've had her here, hiding her for hours and hours, and *now* they decide to move her? When the Russian plane is just about to land? Why would they do that except to make us turn our heads the wrong way and miss the real show?"

"Someone other than us must have thought of that," he says, looking around.

There are definitely fewer armed persons around. If this is the bad guys' plan, it's worked.

"I'm sure some of them have. But at least half of the thinking people have just run out that door. The plane is landing in four or five minutes. Come on," I say. "They said we'd be able to wave at the pilot from the lounge. We might as well have a front-row seat."

We head back to the lounge and take a seat by the window. There are only two other agents still there. They're in the same spots we last saw them in. They raise their heads and acknowledge us.

"Any news about the cellphone?" I ask.

They exchange a quick look. "They caught up to it on the highway. It's Marion's phone, but she wasn't with it."

"Who was?"

"No one," he tells me sheepishly. "The limo that was carrying it was empty except for the driver and the box he was hired to take to Truro. The poor guy is in shock. They're bringing the phone, the car, and the driver back here. They're checking the car to make sure it doesn't have a bomb first."

I turn back to the window. Brian chuckles beside me, breaking into my thoughts.

"Look at that poor guy," he says pointing out the window. "I guess he's just learning how to drive."

I look where he's pointing. A baggage cart is slowly making its way down the little painted road used by the vehicles that service the airplanes. It's jerking and crunching together like an accordion as the little truck that hauls the train of baggage carts leaps ahead in fits and starts. The driver stops the car and steps out in front of us.

"Look at his shoes," I hiss at Brian. "They're shiny black business shoes. What baggage handler wears dress shoes to work?" We're out of our seats and on the move again before I've finished my sentence. My voice gets louder as I try to alert the others in the room.

"Call security!" I scream as we burst from the lounge and head down the hall. We whip around the corner and head to the arrivals area. Running past the rows of seats, we turn a second corner and are faced with a big wall, one door, two guards, and a bunch of baggage carousels.

"How do we get out there, if there are guards at the door?" I bark. "We'll never be able to talk our way past them."

The guard grabs the walkie-talkie off his hip and lifts it to his ear. He's looking right at us.

"This way," Brian calls, grabbing my shirt and pulling me along after him. He runs straight to the nearest baggage carousel. He slows down a little as he jumps up on the conveyer belt, ducks his head, and charges through the plastic curtain that the bags magically appear through.

I hear an authoritative voice yell at us to stop, just before I smash my way through the curtains. Whoever's yelling, I hope they follow us.

The other side is grey cement, steel shelves, and floodlights. By the time I bring my head up from under the curtain, Brian has already started running. "Hey! Hey you!" Brian yells. "Stop right there!"

Two baggage handlers look up from where they're loading bags onto racks. They have work boots on. I ignore them.

The man with the shiny black shoes looks quickly in both directions. Then he takes off running, away from Brian and towards the departures terminal. Brian is running full speed and gaining fast. I take off after them both.

A security guard climbs awkwardly through the plastic curtain behind me and yells "Freeze!" with authority. A steel door ahead of us crashes open and two soldiers charge through it, holding weapons out and at the ready. They yell too, an identically frightening "Freeze!"

It's three to one and at least two of them have guns. I obey and come to a skidding halt.

"Catch that man!" I try to yell to them so they'll hear me over their own repeated yelling and the increasing roar of the airplane that is descending out of the sky at this exact second. "He's not a real baggage handler! He brought the baggage cart! There's a bomb in the cart!"

"Bomb" at an airport is a magic word. Even whispering the word during a calm lull will send airport staff off the deep end. With the Russian president's airplane trying to land beside us, it creates overdrive. Everyone's frantically calling in reinforcements over their walkie-talkies.

One soldier takes off at full speed after Brian and the man with the nice shoes. The other soldier grimly descends on me, grabbing me by the back of my head and throwing me to the ground. He plants his heavy knee in the middle of my back, pinning me to the cement. He pats me down in every direction possible and screams at me to clasp my hands behind my head.

I obey. The roar of the approaching aircraft is almost deafening. Two more soldiers burst in through the steel door. It's loud enough I can't hear it slam against the wall.

I take my hand off the back of my head long enough to point at the baggage cart. *"The cart! Check the baggage cart! Please!!"* I scream, trying to be heard over the airplane engines.

The man on my back stays there, but the security guard and one of the newly arrived soldiers run to the little truck that pulls the baggage carts. One man bravely hops in, cranks the wheel, and pulls it into gear. It is sitting exactly where the president's plane will be parking at any moment. From here it could blow up the plane, the president, and half the airport.

The second soldier runs beside it, helping crank the wheel and pushing the heavy truck into action. It jerks and bucks as it turns towards the runway, aiming for the safety of the open fields on the far side of the landing strip.

A fire alarm sounds from somewhere inside the airport. Not like the polite fire alarm at school, but an ear-splitting scream.

The air pressure is changing with the approach of

the airplane. Wind starts to swirl around the floor by my face. Dust and dirt are kicking up and getting in my eyes. I'm too afraid to blink. Instead, I just pinch my eyes half closed to try to block some of the stinging from the dirt.

More soldiers are pouring out through the door. The two men steering the baggage cart continue to drive it away from us all, offering up their lives to try to save us. It chugs away far too slowly. I will it in my heart to speed up. I know it won't make it all the way across the runway before that big plane touches down.

They're on a collision course.

But suddenly the sound of the engines from the approaching airplane changes. It goes from a dull, body-shaking roar as the engines fight to break against the air and slow the plane down, and instantly becomes a high-pitched whine.

The pilot has hit the gas!

He's pulling up!

They're aborting the landing. They're trying to take off again, and the engines are shrieking even louder than the screaming of the alarms as they try to reverse their slowing trend and fight to once again rise into the air and away from danger.

The wind from the plane becomes a full-force gale. I should turn my head away, but I have to see if the plane will hit the baggage cart, which is now exactly in the middle of its path. The two soldiers either jump or are blown off the truck by the powerful gusts of wind. They roll and tumble for ages before stopping flat on their stomachs on the runway. They freeze there.

The people around me seem to freeze too. I don't look, but I can sense that everyone is holding their breath.

From my place on the floor, I have a frightening side view of the plane as it passes by us. The nose of the plane easily clears the cart. It's banking up hard in a steep climb already. But the landing gear is still down and it looks like it's barely inches above the cart. The moments feel like hours.

It clears!

The second the wings pass over the baggage cart, the blast of air coming out of the back of the engines hits the cart with unimaginable force. The jet's exhaust has enough wind power to pick up the baggage carts and tip them onto their sides, then roll them over. Instead of suitcases, half a dozen five-gallon water bottles spill from the baggage carts and start to tumble down the landing strip.

The truck is lifted as well, and the bottles, the carts, and the truck all tumble, rolling and breaking apart from one another. They scatter like a handful of Lego being thrown at a brick wall and start bouncing end for end down the runway, some water bottles exploding, the carts twisting, and the truck bursting into pieces. Finally the rolling and sliding come to a stop in the grassy edge on the far side.

The plane mounts into the sky with a deafening roar, banks hard over the airport, and disappears from view. Once it passes overtop of the building, the sound is partially blocked and all becomes quieter, almost calm.

I lower my cheek to the dirty cement, close my eyes, and heave a sigh of relief. I release the breath I didn't know I've been holding.

Then the baggage cart explodes with a flash bright enough that I can see it through my closed lids.

It makes me jump half out of my skin. My whole body jerks and tries to curl up into a protective ball. The soldier, still with his knee in my back, throws himself forward to cover me with his body, his two hands over my head. His weight is crushing.

The sound of the explosion hits us with a *fwump*. Peeking out through the really large fingers that are shielding my face, I watch the smoke start from below the truck and grow out and up. It billows in all directions as a huge black cloud of burning gasoline and plastic.

Nothing happens and no one moves for four or five more seconds. There is no second blast. This seems to be over, for now.

"You okay, kid?" the soldier asks after a moment. I would nod, but his hands are still pinning my head to the ground.

"Yeah, I'm good," I answer with a shaky voice.

He tousles my hair like I'm a toddler and climbs off me. He offers me his hand and pops me up off the ground like I'm a bag of bread. I look around hoping someone I know will show up and I can stop feeling like this guy is about to eat me for lunch.

In a few minutes, the roar of the engine is completely gone, but the scream of the fire alarm is still coming from inside the airport. I stand with the soldier and we watch as the fire trucks arrive, sirens blaring, and start hosing down the smoking baggage cart. There really is a lot of smoke.

My head is starting to hurt. Perhaps from the noise, or the smoke, or the stress of everything, but it really is starting to pound.

"I need to find my friend," I tell him, hoping to sound polite.

He scowls at me. "You and your friend took a huge risk, leaving the main terminal and coming into the baggage area. You're lucky we didn't shoot you."

The soldier nudges me towards the door he came through earlier. There's a steady flow of army, police, and security personnel pouring through it. The flow stops briefly and a hole in their parade reveals Brian.

He's at the door, waiting to walk through it into the main part of the terminal. He hasn't seen me. His hands are behind his head.

With a nudge from my keeper's elbow, I understand that I too am supposed to head that way. I'm not sure if I should put my hands behind my head or not. I start to raise them, then lower them, then start to raise them again. Finally, with no clue from my soldier, I decide to jam them into my pockets instead and start walking towards the service door.

Then I see *him*, a few feet behind Brian. The man in the shiny black shoes. He looks a little worse for wear. His hands are behind his head, and clutched between his fingers is a little red book—a Russian passport.

There's a soldier on either side of him, escorting him out of the baggage area and into the main terminal. He doesn't seem intimidated. He looks young, defiant, and angry. He can't be much older than twenty-five, and still he's brave enough to walk along yelling angrily and making smug faces at every armed man he sees.

He's either brave, stupid, or he knows something we don't.

CHAPTER 10

Apparently the Halifax airport has a jail and interrogations rooms. Who knew? They're in the international arrivals area. The nice solider who shoved his knee into my back earlier walks me to a white room with one table, two chairs, and a huge mirror on one wall. He leaves.

I fight the urge to wave at whoever's on the other side of the mirror. Mom doesn't sell them, but I know a two-way mirror when I'm locked in a room with one. It's hard not to look in the mirror. It makes me self-conscious. The easiest way to get around that is to turn my back on it. I move my chair around so I am facing the other wall. With nothing to do but sit and wait, I cross my arms on the table and rest my pounding head.

The click of the door alerts me that someone has arrived. I lift my head and watch as seven people walk into my little white room and circle both the table and me. There are five strangers in suits and uniforms and two pale but familiar faces. Dad looks like he has a bad case of the flu and Jack doesn't look much better. Dad doesn't touch me or speak to me but closes his eyes, listens, and breathes deeply through his nose.

They ask me questions and I answer them. No, I did not know the guy in the shiny black shoes. No, I have no idea what his plans were. Yes, I realize I broke the law by going into the secure area of the airport but I didn't think we had time to do it any other way. Yes, I understand the entire airport is now shut down while they sweep it completely for any additional bombs and that all the flights are either cancelled or redirected to different airports. Yes, I'm a little sorry about that.

I wonder how much more trouble I'll be in if I remind them that if it weren't for Brian and me the airport would already be blown up. I assume it would be like interrupting Mom in the middle of her "Your room is a mess" speech to say "Yeah, so? The garage is a mess too." I always end up cleaning my room AND the garage. It's probably best if I just shut up and take my lumps. An idea pops into my head and I interrupt their questions.

"Dad," I say. He opens his eyes but says nothing. "Does that mean the G8 summit is cancelled? They don't have a place to meet anymore and if the planes can't even land here, there's no way they can continue with the summit. They'll let Mom go, right?"

The entire room drops into silence around me. Like a flock of birds, the adults in the room shift directions and stop being interrogators and start being parents who are looking at a kid whose mother is missing, being held hostage, and in danger.

"I think we're done here," one of the men in suits announces after he clears his throat. "Mr. Johnston, you may take your boy and his friend now, but please stay someplace where we can reach you if we have any more questions." He turns to me.

"Young man," he says. "What you did was stupid beyond compare. You could easily have been hurt or worse." He pauses to scowl at me. "It was also extremely brave. You and your friend were braver than most adults would have been and you may well have saved the life of the Russian president. On behalf of the Airport Authority, we thank you." He steps forward and shoves his hand out towards me. I take his hand after a confused moment and shake it. One by one, the five strangers file out, each of them pausing to shake my hand on the way.

Jack is the second-last to leave. His eyes are red and watery. His handshake is cut short by a quick hug. It lasts only a few moments before he releases me, nods at Dad, and disappears along with the others.

Dad grinds his teeth and looks at me without any expression. He is still white, but I can't tell if its anger, fear, pride, or if he's honestly just sick. He does not shake my hand like the others. He reaches out, pulls me in, and hugs me, just like he used to when I was little—a great big two-armed hug.

After several seconds Dad lets go, grabs the door, and holds it open for me. He walks me to the front door of the Air Canada Executive Lounge. He stops and faces me. The fire alarms are off now, thankfully.

"The airport is the safest place for you and Brian right now," he says. "I don't have time to take you home. Not if I want to get back to Shearwater before the rest of the planes start landing. Whatever it is they were planning for the airport, it's been cut short. They are moving all the incoming planes to Shearwater, and whoever took your mother will want her where the action is. There are no extra people right now, so sit tight until I can get someone to take you back home."

I wonder if Dad has forgotten about the man tied up on our back deck, but decide it's better that I don't ask about that right now. Perhaps someone has gone to get him already, untied him and taken him away. Maybe they've had time to replace the back door, clean up the broken glass, figure out where the power line to the house was cut, and repair that too.

Yes, it's best to leave that conversation where it is for now.

"There are no planes coming in," he continues to explain, "and the whole airport is Code Red. It's safest for everyone if you and Brian stay right here. I absolutely command you to stay put. You will not leave this room for anything other than a bathroom break."

I start to object, but he cuts me off. "I know you don't like to be left out, but I can't handle you being involved in this anymore. This is way too dangerous for a thirteen-year-old, I don't know what I was thinking. You'll be the first person to hear any news as it comes in. I will keep you posted. You're the first person on my speed dial, as soon as I hear *anything*."

We lock eyes. I do not want to be stuck here in the airport while everything is happening someplace else. I can sense my father's tension and don't want to add to it, but I have no intention of staying put like a little kid who's been ordered to stay in his room.

"Promise you won't go anywhere," he says, staring at me.

"I don't have any money, and I'm not old enough to drive." I say, hoping he doesn't notice I'm not promising anything.

He nods like I'm agreeing with him, pats my shoulder, and leaves me at the door.

Inside, Brian is already seated and has found a muffin. His cheek bulges as he smiles at me.

"We're heroes, man!" he garbles through his muffin.

"Get up, hero, it's time to go," I tell him.

"Go where?" he says through his mouth full of food, sitting up straight. "Your dad told me to stay put." He swallows his muffin in a giant lump and clears his throat. "Where do you think we should go, and how exactly are we going to get there? We still don't have any cash."

"Yes, but I have my cellphone," I answer, pulling it out of my pocket. I hit redial. My favourite reporter answers on the second ring.

"Krista Armstrong!" she says in my ear like an overexcited terrier about to go for its first walk in a week.

"Ms. Armstrong, have I got a deal for you!" I tell her with as much enthusiasm as I can fake. I feel a bit like a game show host.

"I'm in!" she practically jumps through the phone. I can hear the excitement in her voice. She's almost bubbling over with it. "Whatever you want, kid, I'm in. You're the kind of news source a reporter can only dream about."

"Where are you?"

"We're still here at the airport. They pushed us all back away from the main building. We're close to the long-term parking. Where are you?"

"Command headquarters," I tell her, trying to make my voice a little deeper and more important sounding. This would not be a good time for it to squeak up five octaves. "We're still inside the terminal." My voice remains that of an important news source and thankfully does not become that of a five-year-old girl being chased by a spider.

She gasps hard into the phone. "Can you get us in?" she hisses in a hopeful whisper.

I have a second of panic. If she gets in here, she'll know I am a fraud. Then she won't take us anywhere.

"No, the story here is over. We're all pulling out and going to the next site. Brian and I need a lift."

"Were you inside when the explosion happened?"

"Sort of…" I answer. I was kind of half in and half out, I guess.

"Do you know what happened? They aren't telling us anything. Will I get an exclusive story out of it?" she asks. I can see her in my mind, her eyebrows pinched together and her eyes focused, like a terrier on the scent trail of a nice, juicy rabbit, and she's hungry for lunch.

"I haven't let you down yet, have I?" I pause for effect. I hope it works. "So is it a deal? Will you give us a lift?"

"Deal," she confirms. "You'll have to come find us, though. They won't let us anywhere near the main building."

"We'll be there in ten. Leave the back door opened a little. We don't want to attract any attention." We both hang up.

Brian is smiling at me. He only heard half the conversation, but it was enough for him to know we are on the case again. There are a few people in the room. Every one of them is ignoring us. They're all typing at their computers or talking into microphones or telephones. I grab our bag, put Mom's computer back inside it, and walk out the front door with Brian as if we're leaving a shopping mall.

A few people look over at us from their security posts as we leave the building and walk out to the sidewalk. We smile casually and just keep moving, all the way around the main parking lots, past long-term parking, and across the road to the Park-N-Fly.

There are six news vans gathered there. Reporters, camera operators, and sound technicians stand in small groups asking each other questions that none of them can answer. They spy us and run over. Lights come on and microphones are shoved into our faces for the second time today.

Brian and I glance at one another. "We're just delivering pizza," Brian tells them. They completely ignore his claim of ignorance and fire questions at us like bullets from a machine gun. They block our path, but we politely try to get past them, repeating that we have no idea what happened inside the airport.

We keep working them back and in the direction of the vans. It's easy to find the van we want. It has a tall blonde waving at us from the back, yelling far too loudly for the distance between us.

"Over here, boys!" she hollers expectantly. "Give them some space, people!" she barks at the rest of them. "Let them through!"

Jaws drop, but they let us pass. As we start climbing into the van, one of the reporters comes back to life.

"Is there a story here, Krista? Should we be following you?" he asks.

Krista shrugs and smiles like Miss America. She gives them all a royal wave but says nothing.

"Come on, we all work the same job here," a second reporter yells. "What have you got?" Krista shuts the door on them and turns to smile at us. She's the cat with the canary.

"Where to now, boys?" she glows greedily.

"The Shearwater military base," I tell her. "It's on the Dartmouth side of the harbour."

"Why Shearwater?" both Brian and Krista ask at the same time.

"Because that's where all the diplomats are being rerouted to. The G8 summit is still on. They're too hard to organize to cancel that easily. They won't give in to terrorists. They're just moving it to a controlled and very secure military base."

Krista's jaw drops. She slides back in her seat and stares at me. "This story has 'Emmy Award' written all over it," she says in wonder.

"Ms. Armstrong," Brian says, interrupting her daydream, "you can't break this story until all the leaders have landed safely, or you will be in direct violation of the national security code section 303-A."

I chance a glace at Brian. We both know there is no national security code section 303-A. He's just making it up. I hope she doesn't know it.

"You can go to jail for that," he adds, nodding knowingly.

"But I have to report the story," she whines. "I'm a reporter! The people have a right to know," she adds with a defiant flick of her fluffed-out hair. She looks undecided and unconvinced.

"Yes, and they can know, but not until after it's all over." Brian has won. "You're the only reporter who has this story, so it's safe. You just have to wait a few extra hours to tell the world what you've learned or we won't be able to tell you anything. You have to promise. You have to give us your word."

"A few hours won't make that much of a difference," she concedes. "Everyone who counts is in bed anyway…if we release the story now, we'd only catch the late news on the West Coast. We are Atlantic Standard Time." Her eyes light up. "I can break the story for the morning news! That would get way bigger coverage! And no one can steal the story overnight!" She nods at us, happy again. "Okay, you have until 7:30 a.m. No later. I look better in the morning light anyway."

We nod back. I look at my watch. It's 1:30 a.m. now. That gives us six hours. It's as close to a promise as you'll ever get out of a news-hungry reporter. We'll have to work with it.

"So, tell me about the airport. What happened there?" She scoots forward in her seat and puts the recorder between us.

I turn to Brian. He was so good with the last story; I can only hope he can come up with another one. My mind is too full of questions, of worry for my mother, to come up with feasible stories. He doesn't let me down. He slides forward and leans in towards her. She responds by leaning in close to him, her recorder inching up between them.

"Russian protesters," he tells her. "I think they're here to protest the poisoning of Lake Baikal. You've heard of Lake Baikal, haven't you?" he pushes her.

Her eyebrows raise and she nods her head, but I can tell she hasn't got a clue. Brian has her on the defensive. It's hard to ask questions about something she's never even heard about. He continues.

"Lake Baikal is the deepest and oldest lake in the world and it's located in the northern part of Russia. The government has used it as a toxic dump for years and years. The lake is getting warmer and more poisonous. It's dying. The protesters have protested. The government agrees. Still, nothing is being done to save the lake. That is," he pauses, "until now."

Barry drives and I listen as Brian weaves a tale about Russian protesters trying to embarrass the Russian government by contaminating the Halifax airport with dirty water from Lake Baikal.

"The dirty lake water ended up all over the runway. But no one knew what was spilled, so the planes couldn't land there until they found out if the fluid was safe or not. It could have been poisoned, or flammable, or anything, really. Imagine what will happen when the media finds out that the world's leaders were afraid to land on water from the Jewel of Russia."

"So Russia has jewels?" she asks.

"No," he tells her. "The 'Jewel of Russia' is the nickname for Lake Baikal because it's so sparkly and blue." He blinks at her and finally adds, "Don't you ever watch the Discovery Channel?"

I almost laugh out loud.

"And they just told you all this while you were in there?" she asks sceptically.

"No!" he scoffs. "I was having my face jammed into the pavement three feet away from the guy when they took him down. He wouldn't lay still. He just kept trying to smack the guards with his passport and yelling at them in Russian."

"You speak Russian?"

"No, but 'jewbell ka Russia', is pretty easy to translate into 'Jewel of Russia.' Put that together with the fifty gallons of water all over the place and it isn't hard to figure out."

I stare at my friend in amazement. He'd been in a different spot from me at the airport, so he had different information, and I'm not completely clear on how much of his story is fiction. I turn my attention to my backpack and pull out my mother's laptop. We're getting close to the military base. I decide to look up a map to see how close we can get to the actual runway. The second the screen comes to life, an icon pops up. A tiny blue bird.

My heart jumps in my chest. A "bird" is the code name for a tracking transmitter. A "bird dog" is the receiver used to hunt the bird down. You can track dozens of birds at a time if you want to. If I have a blue bird on my screen it can only mean one thing.

My mother is close by.

She's the only person who would be transmitting a tracking signal close by and on a frequency that this computer would be listening for.

I click on the mapping icon and a map pops up. I literally hold my breath. It takes forever to load. I wait and wait and wait. Five seconds feels like five hours. Finally, the screen changes and the map appears.

A list of active birds appears at the top of the screen. There is one blue bird flashing. I click on it and all its information pops up. This transmitter is an alarm transmitter. It is RF only, so it's only a Radio Frequency beep. It has no GPS abilities, so it won't be able to give me a dot on the map, just a radar direction relative to where I am.

I square myself up with the front of the car so the computer and I are both facing forwards. Then I click on the map of the world and zoom in until I have found Nova Scotia, then Dartmouth, and finally the road we are travelling on. I pick up a car icon from the side menu and put it on the road where we are, then drag the car to show the direction we're going.

"Stop!" I yell. Barry doesn't stop right away. Instead, he looks back to see if Krista agrees.

"Stop now! Right now! Now! Now! Now!" I yell. Whether she agrees or not, he obeys my urgent demand and pulls over on the side of the street.

Instead of giving me a GPS dot on a map, the best this alarm transmitter can do is give me a general direction. The map is mostly green, brown, and white, but a blue wedge shape appears. The point of the wedge is over top of my car icon and it spreads out wider and wider in the direction of the harbour.

"We're on the wrong side of the harbour," I tell them. My mother is still in Halifax—or at the very least, her alarm is. Everyone in the van had been silent since my outburst. I ignore the others and look up at Brian.

"I've got her," I whisper, almost unable to speak, tears squeezing at the corner of my eyes.

"Where?" he asks, scooting over to see the screen.

He understands everything the second he sees the screen and the wedge. "The alarm pen's in her purse," he says.

I nod.

"Change of plans, Krista," Brian says. "We need to make a slight detour to Halifax."

"Why?" Krista asks all breathless and excited. She leans around so she can look at my computer screen too. It doesn't mean anything to her. It's just a map of Dartmouth with a blue piece in it.

"Should we call Jack and Dad?" I ask Brian, completely ignoring Krista as she tries desperately to figure out what we're so excited about on the screen.

"It might be her," he nods, "but it might be one of the transmitters from your bag too. It could have fallen out at the Citadel when you were being tossed around. What if someone just picked it up during the cleanup and thought it looked like a regular pen and pushed the little button top to see if the pen works? The alarm would have started transmitting and they never would have known."

I stare at the screen. He's right.

"There is no point in distracting them from what they are doing in Shearwater if all they are hunting down is a lost pen. It's a ten-minute drive. Let's wait until we're over there and see before we let your dad know you broke your promise to stay put."

"It's a technicality, but I never promised to stay put. I told him I didn't have any money."

"Yeah, that'll save ya, man." He rolls his eyes. "Good defence. You should stick to it."

"Why are we heading to Halifax?" Krista interrupts.

"To get you an Oscar to go with your Emmy, maybe even a Golden Globe and the keys to the Emerald City," Brian answers. "You're going to have to trust us. This is all one story and it's big."

"How big?" she asks eagerly.

"This story is bigger than the airport story and bigger than the bombing of the Old Town Clock," Brian tells her.

"Turn the van around," she barks at the driver. "We're heading to Halifax."

The signal fades and disappears the further we drive. It's completely gone as we drive over the bridge that connects Dartmouth and Halifax. We've driven too far away to be able to pick up the signal, but the bridge is the only way to get to the other side. Heading up Lower Water Street, we try to avoid the mess and confusion still going on up at the Citadel. The signal fades back in the closer we get to the downtown core of the city.

I ask Barry to stop at the bottom of the hill, below

where the clock tower once stood. Looking out the passenger window I can see work crews and police and fire engine lights, but most of the people have gone home. Out the driver's side window I can see the harbour. It's a mostly calm night, and the water is smooth and black.

I place our car icon on the map at our new location by the waterfront, dragging the icon to show what direction the car is moving.

The blue wedge appears. I'm still half expecting to find it pointing to the Citadel, but it's facing out towards the harbour and Dartmouth on the other side. I stare, dumbfounded.

"How could that be?" I ask Brian, pointing at the screen. "We just left there."

He looks at the screen, then out through the window in the direction the little wedge tells us my mother is.

"In a boat in the harbour?" he suggests with a shrug.

Leaning forward to tap Barry on the shoulder I ask, "How strong are those lights on your camera?"

"Powerful enough to see a boat in the harbour, if that's what you're asking." He has not spoken once in all the time we've been together, but apparently he's been listening.

"Let's go."

Brian and I pull on our bulletproof vests like it

is second nature. We all climb out—Krista with her handheld microphone, Barry with his camera, Brian with the backpack, and me with the laptop. We walk towards the docks. Everything is quiet. The yachts and sailboats and smaller motorboats are all tied up peacefully against the wooden pier. The water is so calm that they don't even rock.

"Take a peek out that way," I tell Barry, pointing out at the empty harbour. "Let's see if there's anything out there."

The floodlight on the top of the camera comes to life and shines out over the water. Barry pans left and right several times, but there are no boats moving, and nothing to see except the far shore of Dartmouth, which we have just left.

I check the map again. From down here by the water, there are fewer things to get in the way of the signal. The signal is strong, so we can't be that far away. The wedge has shifted a few degrees. It's pointing towards Dartmouth and the mouth of the harbour.

I follow the lights of the Dartmouth waterfront along to the refinery, which glows brightly. The lights disappear behind McNabs Island, and on the other side the lights from Shearwater's military base appear.

I tap the screen for Brain. He looks and nods. If

she's not in Halifax and she's not in Dartmouth and there are no boats, it makes perfect sense. I grab my cellphone and dial. Dad answers on the second ring.

"She's on McNabs Island, Dad," I tell him. It makes me shiver to look out at the black, uninhabited lump in the harbour that is McNabs Island, and know my mother is on it.

"What's happened?" he asks. "What makes you think she's on McNabs? There's nothing on McNabs."

"What better place to hide something, than in a place where there's no one to see it? It has a view of the Citadel on one side and Shearwater on the other. Dad, it's the perfect place for them. If they've got radio boosters, they'll be within radio range for either place. They'll also have a perfect view of each airplane's belly as they come in to land. Besides, I've picked up one of her disguised alarm pens."

"Sweet roses in June," my father cusses and lets out a long low whistle as he digests what I have just told him.

A yell comes from one of the boats. I'm not paying attention, but apparently our lights are keeping the boaters awake. One is topside and addressing us sharply. Brian goes to try to make peace."

"It makes sense," Dad says quickly, having processed what I've said. "I'll pass your thoughts on to the others and call you back."

"Dad, I'm not at the airport," I confess.

"I didn't really expect you would be," he sighs, "but I was hoping. I'll call you back when we get a plan together." We disconnect.

Brian waves at me from the deck of the boat the protester emerged from. I watch as Barry and Krista climb aboard and shake hands with the owner. They too wave me over.

Brian greets me as I climb down into the boat.

"This is my partner, Andrew Johnston," he says pointing at me. Then, turning to point at the man who is now shaking my hand, he continues. "I was just explaining how we're one of the teams on a reality TV show, where contestants have two weeks to travel all over the world, following branches of their family tree to see which one of us has the most important relatives. I was telling Mr. Rafuse here about how we have to prove that one of our uncles was a general in the American army and how he heroically fought here, on McNabs Island, during the war of 1812.

"Mr. Rafuse understands that the contest closes tomorrow morning at nine, New York time. He thinks it's exciting that NBC has sent their own news crew to cover the event, because it is such a tight race for first place, and that if he helps us and we win, he's sure to be on network TV by lunchtime tomorrow." Brian smiles big and wide, his eyes bulging at me.

Barry and Krista are both nodding vigorously at me in hopes that I'll understand the lie and play along.

I do. I've been a liar for years and years. Mr. Rafuse finishes shaking my hand and congratulating me on having done so well in this race. He tells me to call him Ken, and then he sets about unfastening the boat from the dock and shoving off. It amazes me what people will do for you if you spin it the right way.

In just a few minutes, Ken cuts the engine and we glide up to the wooden dock on the Halifax side of McNabs Island. I hop out first, grab the line he throws me, and help him tie the boat up. The others make their way off the boat as well and we all head up off the dock. It's a bit of an odd crew.

Ken is trotting along happily, assuming he's living out the adventure of a reality show. Barry has the camera up and at the ready on his shoulder, peering at the world from behind his lens. Brian and I are scanning the shoreline and hilltop, looking for movement, and Krista...she's skittering along the dew-covered boards in her high-heeled boots, going from person to person, peeking out from behind us with her microphone held out in front of her like a flashlight or a loaded gun.

My pocket rings. It makes me jump.

"We're going to find some people to spare and send them out to have a look around. Things are a little crazy around here. We're going off in a hundred different directions, now that they've changed airports and the location for the meetings," my father tells me. "Whatever you do, just stay away from the island."

"Dad?" I try to interrupt, but he cuts me off before I can get a word in.

"You're already there, aren't you?"

We're both silent.

"You've left the airport, made your way to Halifax, and you're already on the island, aren't you?"

"Yup."

"Seriously, Andrew!" he exclaims. "Can't you have problems like a normal teenager? Can't we just get a call from the school because you're skipping class or something? There are a hundred people trying to find your mother and keep these stupid politicians alive, and you and Brian end up out on an island with some political extremists trying to overthrow the Russian president."

"Really?" I say, taken back a bit. "Brian has a

theory about them being environmentalists."

"They're not. Do I at least get to tell you that much? Can we know *that much* that you don't already know?" There is sarcasm dripping in his voice. "It's a cover. They want to make it look like that so that when they assassinate the president and take over, the Russian people won't object. Heaven help us all if they succeed."

I don't know what to say. I'm here and we both know I'm not leaving.

"Be *careful*, and keep your head down." He sounds frustrated. "Will you at least do *that* for me? Stay out of sight until we get there?"

"Yes, Dad," I say with a smile. "I promise to be careful. But you don't have to worry." I glance over at Krista, hiding behind the man with a camera for a head and the happy, adventure-seeking boat owner, "I have adult supervision."

CHAPTER 11

My spidey senses go off like a cannon. This is too easy. My foot freezes in mid-stride when we reach the end of the dock. I flash my hands out on both sides of me, like a human barricade, to stop the others from going any further. If the people we're looking for are on this island, they absolutely know about this dock. There are only three places where you can get off a boat and onto McNabs Island, and if they're hiding here, they'll be interested in knowing when company comes.

Brian looks around first, trying to spot the danger.

"Electronic guards," I whisper. The others look all around as if a shiny steel robot is going to step forward and say, "Halt! Who goes there?"

"Krista," I ask, turning towards her but keeping my hands up as a barrier, "do you have any hairspray in your gym bag?"

"In this?" she whispers, hoisting up her gigantic black bag.

I nod.

"This is my *purse*! Of course I have hairspray in my *purse*." She clutches the bag to her chest. "Why?"

"I need to borrow a little squirt of it, please," I tell her, dropping one of my hands from its road-blocker position and reaching out towards her. She hesitates for a second, but gives in, rummages through her bag, and hands me a huge bottle of hairspray.

Pointing the nozzle away from us and towards the shore, I press the button and draw a straight line in the air that starts at my head and ends at the ground. It makes a white mist in the moonlight, but that's it.

Brian nods his head knowingly, but the three others look at me like I've lost my mind. I start to walk forward, but Brian grabs my arm.

"It might be on a strobe," he says. "To save power. They'd probably need to use it out here 'cause they've got no place to plug in."

I hadn't thought of that. We count ten seconds, then Brian and I step forward towards where the dock ends and the rocky shore begins. The others follow in behind us like ducklings behind their mother. We all stop and I spray the air again. Krista grabs me by the shoulders and cranes her neck around me to see what's happening. We count and wait.

Nothing happens—the misty spray just hovers, then drifts to the ground.

"I'd say once we get off the dock we're clear," Brian suggests.

"This should be it, then," I answer, looking down at the threshold between wood and rocks. This time I spray the mist in a giant S-shape that starts at my head and ends at my toes. We start the count.

"One Mississippi, two Mississippi, three—" A perfectly straight, bright red line appears at hip level. It sparkles as the hairspray falls through it, picking up and redirecting fragments of the laser light as the spray flutters down to the ground. The three people behind us gasp in unison.

"Keep counting," Brian says overtop of their collective gasping. I agree and we continue.

"Four Mississippi, five Mississippi, six Mississippi—"

The beam vanishes, and still we count.

"Seven Mississippi, eight Mississippi, nine Mississippi."

It reappears. We stop counting because we have the pattern: three seconds on and three seconds off.

"Can we get that on film?" Krista asks in an urgent whisper.

"Sure," I tell her. "Lasers and hairspray aren't

classified equipment. Film away, but don't touch it, or we're all in trouble." Turning to Ken, I add, "Perhaps you should stay here and guard the boat instead of coming with us. Someone from the other team might come by and try to take the boat so they can win. I'd hate to see you lose your boat."

Ken nods and steps back, looking a little disappointed.

"Should we get Krista and Barry to stay here and wait as well?" Brian asks quietly in my ear. I shake my head and pull him off to the side.

"That camera is the best weapon we've got. No one wants to get caught on tape breaking the law. You can't argue with video evidence. It won't make us invincible, but it's as good a safety tool as these bullet-proof vests." I pat my vest for emphasis. He nods and I step back, making sure to smile at Krista.

I spray the air again. Barry has hoisted the camera onto his shoulder. Krista automatically pats at her hair. Without turning the spotlight on, he begins filming. Krista whispers urgently into her microphone and crouches down so both her head and the bright red beam will be in the same shot. When she's finished, we squirt again and all four of us begin counting. The beam reappears.

"Step up, folks," Brian says. "We only have three seconds to get through without setting off the alarm."

The beam blinks out and the four of us quickly step past, way past, two or three strides past just for good measure. I hand the hairspray back to Krista.

The ground is mostly rock, with a few patches of moss and pockets of stunted grass. Krista's high-heeled boots click on the surface of the rocks. Barry drops the heavy camera off his shoulder and we start walking up the hill.

I fill them in on my conversation with my father. We are no longer looking for environmentalists but for a group of people trying to assassinate the Russian president. Krista stumbles along, trying to record everything. Brian shakes his head at how very close his imaginary story has ended up hitting the mark.

"What are we looking for?" she asks.

"Anything," I answer truthfully. "A tent, a boat, people, a small shed—anything that doesn't look like it should be here."

"Should we split up?" she asks.

"No," I tell her, glancing over at Brian. "We need to get to the top of this hill first. We should be able to see something from there. If our guess is right, the people we're looking for will be on the Dartmouth side focusing on Shearwater, and not on us back here on the Halifax side. We might be able to sneak up on them."

With the exception of Krista's boots, we're silent as we make our way up the hill. The closer we get to the top, the farther down Brian and I crouch. Barry follows along no problem, copying our crouched postures as we go, carrying the heavy camera a few inches above the ground. Brian and I repeatedly give Krista hand signals to get her to crouch a bit. She stoops a little and bends her knees a few degrees, but remains dangerously upright.

In the end, Barry just grabs her by the hand and pulls her to her knees.

Krista indignantly flips her hair over her shoulder and tries to crawl along with as much style as a crawling person can muster. Her head is still held high as we crawl over the rough ground and crest the hill. Because she's moving with her head highest in the air, and because she's been trained as a snoopy reporter, she sees it first.

"I see something," she announces excitedly.

"Then get down!" I hiss.

Again, Barry grabs her and hauls her down. She lands on her elbows and looks over at Brian and me for direction. Barry keeps his hold on her to keep her down and looks our way as well. Two thirteen-year-old kids are the leaders.

Getting on our bellies, the four of us commando crawl up the last few feet to the crest of the hill. Keeping as low as possible to remain invisible to whoever's on the other side, we peek over the top.

Below and to the right is a Boy Scout campsite. Seven little white tents are circled around a big dome tent in the middle. There are camping chairs, laundry lines, and a flagpole.

"You brought us here to look at a camp-out?" Krista asks in disgust, crawling back a few inches.

"It looks like a camp-out," Brian explains, "except it's now four o'clock in the morning and there are enough people moving around down there for it to be midday."

She looks again. Barry looks again. Brian and I sit back on our bottoms and think. "To top it off they have guards posted along the perimeter. Most camp-outs don't have guards at the four corners of the camp at four in the morning."

"Why are you two boys out here trying to save the Russian president?" Krista asks suddenly, as though she's only just realized how weird it is.

"They have my mother," I blurt out. "That's why we're here."

Brian looks over at me. For some reason I need to tell the truth.

"That's why we're involved at all. They have my mother and we don't know why, except that she's involved with the security for the G8 summit. Now we're up here, and she's down there, and we have to get her back."

"Are you kidding me?" Barry asks earnestly.

"No," I answer with fear and frustration.. "My dad is with the police and the military. They say they're on their way, but with the G8 summit in town, and all the diplomats flying in, and the airport diverted, everyone is stretched thin. It's hard to find spare people to send out on what could be a whim. They were all already dragged out to the airport because they thought my mom was there."

"If we can create a diversion, it could buy your dad some time to get here with the cavalry, and keep the Russians distracted from their next move," Brian adds. "We've messed with their first two ideas. Who knows how many backup plans they've got?"

"What if they don't need my mother for their next set of plans?" I can feel the panic starting to take over and fight to hold it back. "We are running out of time here. They could do ANYTHING! We have to sneak down this hill and find her. It will be a lot easier to keep my mother safe if we know where she is *before* the cavalry arrives and all hell breaks loose."

"They'll spot us for sure, the second we come over the top of this hill. They've got lookouts posted along the edge of camp and you can be guaranteed they've at least got night-vision goggles!" Brian hisses. "You already saw one pair at the hill. If they had them there, then they'll have them here too."

"We can't turn back now!" I hiss back. "If they have my mother, this is where they've got her! Every minute we wait, she's in more danger."

We're silent for a few moments while we race to think up a plan. Brian is the first to speak.

"Showtime?" he asks, tipping his head towards Krista and Barry. "A little flash and dash, perhaps?" He waggles his eyebrows at me.

"Showtime," I agree with a nod. It's not much of a plan, but it's something.

"Barry," I say, turning towards him. "We're going to need your help for a few minutes. Are you up for it?"

"What do you need?" he asks, firm and honest.

"A distraction and some camouflage. Does your floodlight have an on-off switch that's easy to get at?" I ask.

"Flick of my thumb," he answers, nodding.

"Okay, then. Brian and I are going to circle around the edge of this hill. When you hear us give the signal, turn on the floodlight. Then count five full seconds, and turn it off again. Keep up the pattern, of five on and five off. If they start coming up the hill, run for the boat, don't worry about tripping the alarm at the end of the dock, because they'll already know you're here. Get on the boat and get out of here. Okay? Can you do that?"

"Yes," Barry nods. "I can do that."

"What do you want me to do?" Krista asks eagerly, looking from one of us to the other.

"We need you to keep your head down," Brian answers her.

"But I have to do something!" she protests, flapping her hands.

"Okay, go to the boat now and tell Ken to start the engine," Brian offers, pointing back in the direction of the boat.

"But the story is *here*," she protests. "I need to report this story. It's what I do!"

"We'll give you a full interview after," I say. "We don't know what's going to happen down there. We just want to make sure as few people are involved as possible." I don't tell her that her excitable personality could become a liability around what I assume are a whole bunch of automatic weapons.

"Just keep safe, Krista. Please," Brian tries to persuade her.

"Okay! Okay!" she hisses. "I'll go back down to the boat and stay there until Barry shows up."

"Great. Thanks," he calls quietly after her as she starts to head down the hill. "I promise it will be a great interview when this is all over."

Brian and I move down a few feet ourselves, so we drop out of the line of sight behind the crest of the hill, where we can stand up and move quickly without having to crouch. It takes us only a few minutes to get in place on the other side of the hill. We need to be close enough to Barry that he'll hear us whistle, but far enough away that the people down at the camp won't be able to see us if they're looking his way.

Brian grew up in Chicago; he only knows how to whistle for taxis. I've spent half my life in the woods with my father; I know twenty different birdcalls. Once we're far enough away from Barry, I take a deep breath and imitate the shrill of an Arctic tern. Not that any birds call out at night, but at least it isn't unheard of for terns to be in Halifax Harbour.

Instantly, Barry's floodlight comes on and bathes most of the slope in white light. Brian and I duck our heads and try to shield our eyes from the glare with our arms. We count to five.

On five, the light goes out. We pop up and start running towards the tent village at the bottom. We stay close together, trying to move as one. At the count of five, we both drop into a crouch close to the ground and cover our eyes.

If the people down below are using night-vision goggles, the five-on and five-off pattern will keep them completely blind. If they're not, their naked eyes will have a hard time adjusting to the light changes. It's the best we can do.

Voices erupt from below. We're halfway to the closest tent, close enough hear movement as people spill out of them. The light goes out. We're up and running again, paying close attention to the rocky, uneven ground. One Mississippi, two Mississippi, three Mississippi, the first tent is within reach, four Mississippi, five Mississ—we crouch and cover our eyes.

The light comes on.

"Hello!" we hear a familiar voice ring out in overly happy tones. Abandoning our protective stances, Brian and I both look up and stare. Shock and dismay kick in. I'm a total loss as I watch Krista Armstrong standing in the spotlight at the top of the hill. She waves her handheld microphone in the air like it's a flag as she smiles and starts walking down the hill towards the tents and the building crowd of people around them.

"I'm Krista Armstrong!" she calls ahead of herself, waving excitedly with her free hand. "I'm from the Atlantic Broadcasters Network and we're here on a live feed, which is being sent out to all eight of our sister stations!" Her voice bubbles and pops like she's telling them they've all just won the big prize at the lottery.

A hand yanks at my shoulder. It's Brian. He's already up and on the move again. He half-pulls me to my feet as I watch Krista tiptoeing her way down the hill in her high-heeled boots. She's centred in the spotlight, waving and smiling as if she has every right in the world to be where she is.

The light goes out.

Brian and I dash, mostly blind ourselves from having looked her way, and aim for the closest tent. It's a sealed dome tent, so we can't just peek underneath the sides to see what or who is inside. Skidding to a halt beside the first tent, we creep along the back of it, making our way towards the side and then up near the front, which is facing the centre of the little camp. Just as we reach the front of the tent, the door flap whips open, the zipper barely missing my face. I throw my hand up defensively and catch the edge of the door flap and step back, bumping into Brian.

The light comes on again. People are speaking everywhere in urgent and angry tones, and sharp accents. Above them all, Krista's voice rings out.

"Oh, those crazy cameras!" She laughs in a high-pitched voice. "They're always cutting out. Could I have everyone gather over here for a moment?" She makes circling motions with her hands, beckoning people up the hill towards her. "I'd like you all to get a chance to say hello to our three million viewers. I'm sure they're all really interested to hear what you have to say!"

"She's so *smart*," I whisper to Brian. Because she's just let them know that whatever they do next, it will be broadcast live for the world to see.

I watch a man in khaki pants and a dress shirt running from the tent that has just finished slapping me in the face. He runs towards the centre tent. Some people are pouring out of it and others are racing in. Whatever is going on, it's going on inside that tent.

Ducking my head around the corner, I chance a quick look inside the smaller tent beside me. It has one cot and three laptops, all set up on top of wooden crates. All three screens are up and glowing brightly in the dark tent. The interior walls are all draped with what looks like an aluminium fishing-net fabric. The shiny silver threads glow in the faint computer light.

I back out of the tent and whisper to Brian.

"They've got radio netting," I tell him. "That's why no one knew they were here. All these tents must have it. Whenever the secret service flew a security sweep over the island, they wouldn't have found anything, because these guys are using radio netting to block any signals or communications from getting out!"

Brian points ahead of me towards the centre tent. I look where he's pointing. There are more people running around and a faint rumble is starting to fill the air.

"That's not a normal flagpole, either," he says. "The flags are completely stiff and metal posts are sticking out of the tops of them. They're just disguising antennas."

"Directional antennas," we whisper in unison.

"You need four antennas to get a good direction on a signal," I confirm quietly. "If they're trying to track these airplanes as they come in or take off they'll need at least four antennas to pinpoint them."

"Let's go," Brian says just as the light goes out again.

We know the direction of the tent but run blind for a few strides, hoping not to run into anyone.

Brian gets there first. I can feel him slowing in front of me and I check my stride to match his. The low rumble in the air is getting louder. It sounds like a helicopter.

"Is that one of ours or one of theirs?" Brian hisses over his shoulder.

"I have no idea," I answer, twisting around to try to figure out which direction the sound is coming from.

When the light comes back on I can see Krista. For all her tiptoeing down the hill, she hasn't moved an inch closer. She's spent the whole time tiptoeing on the spot or backing up every time the light goes out. Clever. I wouldn't have thought of it.

There are people moving everywhere, about twenty of them at best guess. Most are moving between the big tent in the middle and the three tents closest to the shoreline. Those tents are only about fifteen feet away from the water. I try frantically to decide which way to go. They're all so busy running that no one seems to be looking our way. Looking around, I see two people getting very near to Krista. I wonder if she'll turn and run, or just stand her ground and fake her way through this.

A flash of guilt streaks through me. If anything happens to Krista or Barry it will be my fault. I'm the one who got them into this. But I can't fix that. I can only tackle one problem at a time. I need to find my mother. Krista and Barry are going to have to be temporarily on their own.

"Over here," Brian hisses.

I follow the sound of his voice. It pulls me back in from my own spinning thoughts. We're in the shadow of the big tent on the far side from Krista and her spotlight. Brian is standing beside a tent, where the clothesline disappears in through a hole. He rubs the line between his fingers then turns to nod at me.

"Its antenna wire," he hisses. "A giant, sixty-foot antenna wire disguised as a clothesline. It's double-stranded, too! One line out and one line back—they can probably hear radio from Africa." He pulls himself up, stretching to his full height, and peeks in through the clothesline opening.

"You've got to be joking!" he exclaims, pulling himself up closer to the hole and pushing his whole face in through the opening.

"What?" I ask. "What is it? Is it her?" I can feel my heart beating faster.

"It's a tank!" he says far too loud.

"A tank of what?" I hiss.

"A tank of *tank*!"

Whump-whump-whump-rooomm sounds from inside the big domed tent, matched by the roar of the approaching helicopter. Actually, helicopters. I can see now that there are two of them. I still don't know if they're ours or theirs, but they are getting closer and louder.

We have to do something. I have to do something. I start running. It's time to meet this thing head-on. No more hiding.

I run around to the front of the large tent, start in through the door, and stop short. I feel like I've run into a brick wall as something slams into my chest and knocks the wind out of me. The flaps of the door spread wide and an honest-to-heavens, real, live tank starts to drive over me. At least, it's a tank on the bottom half. Mounted on the top of it is the cab and box of a dump truck. I realize with shock that I have run into it more than it has run into me.

My hands scramble frantically over the metal face of the tank, trying desperately to find something to grab hold of on the smooth surface, anything that I can use to haul myself upright. The wide, grey metal face of the tank slides past my nose as I sink to the ground beneath it. Then it pushes me over and I stumble back, holding my chest as I fall to the ground. Finally, I am no longer able to keep myself up and in front of the moving wall of metal. I try to suck in some air and crawl backwards away from the advancing vehicle. It's faster than me. I'm losing.

The tank clears the doors with its nose. I am between two huge sets of studded tires. There are six tires on each side. To the left and right of me, the first of two huge tires crunch and grind their way over the rocks and gravel. I can't get out from beneath the tank fast enough. Looking towards my feet, I estimate how much clearance I've got. Between the belly of the tank and the ground I have about two feet to squeeze under.

I only have two choices. I can risk jumping out from between the huge rolling wheels or stay underneath and hope for the best. I flop back flat on the ground, pressing my shoulders tight to the earth as I look up and watch in terror as this giant machine rolls overtop of me. The steel belly of the tank is inches from my nose as it crawls past. Above the grinding and crunching I can hear my friend scream my name.

"I'm good!" I scream back. "I'm good!" I repeat it a few more times, trying to be heard over the crunching of stones, the clacking of gears from the tank and the increasing roar of the approaching helicopters. I'm not sure if I'm trying to convince him or me. My heart is beating wildly in my chest. I've never been driven over by a five-tonne vehicle before. It feels like slow motion. I watch, frozen to the ground, as the last of the six sets of wheels makes its way past me. The sky opens up as the tail of the tank clears my head and rolls away.

I sit up immediately and am hit in the back of the head with the tent doors as they fall back into place in the wake of the tank. It doesn't hurt, but it shocks me. Brian is there before the canvas settles. He grabs my shoulders and helps me to my feet, his hands holding me steady.

We're standing inside a now-deserted tent. There are no people inside and the centre is completely bare. The sides are cramped around the edges with computers, wires, small folding chairs, and wooden crates, just like the smaller tent had been. A huge map of Nova Scotia all but fills one wall. It has dozens of pins stuck into it.

We stare in shock. It's like something out of a James Bond movie.

FAWHOOM!

An explosion from somewhere outside sends a bright flash and a shock wave through the tent walls and us. It jars us back into motion.

"Run!" we both yell, turning on our heels and speeding out of the tent.

Looking over my shoulder, I see that the first tent we peeked into is now a ball of flames. They're destroying anything that could be evidence. The other tents are sure to go up any second as well—if one is wired to blow, they're all wired to blow. This must be part of their emergency plan, much like their evacuation plan at the town clock: Get out, then self-destruct.

Once we clear the tent flaps, I can see the three lower tents have been opened and a dozen two-man Jet Skis are being shoved towards the water. There are two men with each Jet Ski, one on either side. The camp is emptying out. But where is my mother?

Brian and I are both moving forward, towards the water on the Dartmouth side. The same direction the helicopters are coming from. His head is turning from side to side as much as mine must be. Neither of us knows which way to go.

I look up at the helicopters, which are almost overhead, and see that they've backed off. It's hard to fly over updrafts caused by explosions. If the gust of air was enough to rock Brian and me on the ground level, then the added gust caused by the sudden heat and rising air currents would be playing havoc on the helicopter pilots. They've had to move away from the centre of the camp for safety.

The side doors open and four black-clad bodies jump out of each helicopter. Although I can't see the ropes in the dim light, I know by their controlled speed as they come down that they're all on harnesses. They descend quickly and smoothly. I'm still not sure whose side they're on, but I make a quick and silent wish that they are for us, not against us.

A second blast brings my attention back to the camp, and I duck to protect my head with my arms. It's another of the smaller tents. Just as I start to bring my arms down, a third tent goes up in flames. It takes a few seconds before the explosion comes. I don't wait for it. I start for the shore. If everyone else is headed for the water, I need to be there too. Brian is still close beside me.

A sudden scream from Krista interrupts my thoughts. I had forgotten about her completely. Now I can't make out her words. The light from the camera goes out, and if it weren't for the burning tents, everything would be dark. They had turned the lights on full-time to record. If it hadn't been for them recording, the camp would have been dark. Stopping hard, I twist to look back towards the hill. I can only make out movement. I can't see Krista. Brian and I both reach out a hand for one another.

"You go help Krista," I yell, pushing him on his

shoulder and sending him in her direction. "I'm going for Mom." He disappears from underneath my palm as we separate, both running in opposite directions: him up the hill to help Krista, and me towards the water, closer to Dartmouth and away from my friends.

Looking down the hill, I don't really have a plan. The Jet Skis are almost at the water and the tank is about halfway there. Mom's obviously not on one of the Jet Skis; I can see everyone pushing and pulling those.

The only other place she can be—unless she was in one of those exploding tents, which I can't even think about—is the tank. So I aim for the tank as it rolls towards the water. It will have to stop before it gets there. There's no bridge, and no ferry big enough to take it off the island, so it can't go far. I will save my mother.

With all my effort, I make my way towards the tank. The ground is less uneven on this side of the island and running is easier. I hit full speed quickly and hurtle down the hill, barely in control. I close the gap quickly and reach the back of the steel vehicle, slowing just enough to stop from crashing into it.

"Stop!" I scream, but they ignore me. "Let her out! Just *let her out!*" I screech at the top of my voice as I thump the sloping top at the back of the vehicle.

Again, they ignore me. I instantly understand that no matter what I say, they're going to keep rolling.

Desperate not to let her get further away from me, I try to jump up onto the wedge-shaped, smooth back. It's too high. I slide off instantly. Running behind the vehicle, I move to the right rear and jump again, reaching as far up the vehicle as possible, trying to find a handhold. Nothing. My hand just slides over the cold metal as I slip back to the rocky ground.

I side-skip to the left rear of the vehicle and try again, jumping with all my might. My baby finger smacks into something hard before I slide back to the ground again. My heart leaps. At least now I have found something to hang onto, something to leverage myself up with.

I allow the tank to get a step ahead of me, and then I take two running strides before I convert my forward energy into upward energy and jump towards the vehicle as high as I can. My wrist hits a metal bar. It hurts, but I ignore it and hook my fingers to catch the bar as I slide back down.

My fingers catch. My arm straightens as my weight pulls me down and my shoulder is nearly wrenched out of its socket, but I hang on. My feet are dangling in mid-air; I pedal them wildly, trying to get a foothold. There's nothing. Unlocking my elbow, I strain to pull myself up by one arm. Reaching up with my free hand, desperately trying to find something to hang onto, my fingertips find the other end of the metal bar.

Finger by finger, I find my grip around the bar with my second hand. With two hands I can pull myself up, but my feet slip on the steep metal and swing free again and again, over the end of the tank. I'm losing time. There has to be another way.

Looking up towards the truck top of the tank just as the floodlights from one of the helicopters flashes overhead, I can see there is a second bar about fifteen inches higher than the one I'm holding onto now, and there's one more above that. It's a ladder! I use my arms to climb, swinging my legs from side to side to give me momentum. By the time my hands pull me up onto the third bar, my feet can curl underneath me and reach the first. I start to stand and climb at the same time.

The tank jerks to one side, tipping as it rolls over some unseen object. It throws me off balance. My hips swing wildly to the side, but I pull myself back to the metal ladder and keep climbing. I crest the top of the curve and find myself on the deck of a giant truck. There are rows of wooden seats on both sides and a wooden floor. In the middle of the floor is a one-foot-high steel fence in the shape of a circle with an opening on one side. In the middle is a large metal steering wheel.

It's the hatch to get into the belly of the tank.

An explosion cracks the air behind me and I throw myself flat against the wood, reaching for the hatch to hold on to. Arching sideways on my belly, like a lizard chasing its own tail, I look back and see a second flash of light as the large centre tent finally disintegrates into a billion pieces.

The men who have just been dropping out of the helicopters are heading our way. Two of them have dropped to the ground completely. I don't know if they're hurt or just avoiding the shrapnel and compression blast from the explosion. The others are running full speed towards the tank.

I'm sure they'll reach us. The tank has run out of land—it's up against the small wooden dock now. Looking over the camp, I can't see Brian or Krista or Barry anywhere at all. There's too much light and smoke between us now, with all the tent fires.

Turning back towards the front of the tank, I scramble forwards on my hands and knees. Grabbing hold of the hatch on the floor with both hands, I give it a hard crank to the left. It doesn't budge. Nothing at all—not a jerk, not a hint of movement. I might as well be trying to turn a mountain.

I hear the crunch of the wooden dock underneath us. "What are you thinking?" I scream to the driver, even though there's no way he can hear me. "There's no way that dock can hold a tank!"

Realization hits me like a two-by-four over the head. They're going to sink it. They're destroying the evidence and they're going to sink this tank with my mother inside it.

"*No!*" I scream.

Still the tank rolls forward.

I howl a second time, pulling straight up on the latch and looking around frantically for some clue as to what to do next. Banging on the deck with both hands, I scream, "I'm up here, Mom! I'm here! Mom! I'm coming!"

There are lights coming towards us from across the harbour. They're boats coming from the Dartmouth side, dozens of them, judging by the number of lights approaching.

Dad must be in one of those boats, but he'll be too late. They'll all be too late. The tank will be gone long before he gets here. It will fill with water and sink. There will be no way to save Mom.

Behind me, two of the runners are closing in. They could be good guys, but I just don't know. Either way, they won't make it to the tank before it fully enters the water. They'll have to swim to catch up. I have to *do* something. I'm the only one here and I can't budge the hatch. I have to do something else.

"The cab," I say to myself.

Ahead of me is the back of the truck cab. Someone has to be driving this thing. Skirting around the metal fence that protects the hatch, I leap to the front of the seating area. There's nothing but a solid steel wall. No window or door to get into the cab. I climb up on the bench on the passenger side, and, grabbing one of the floodlights on the top of the cab, I use it to lean around to look at the side.

There's a window there, and it's either open or has no glass to begin with. I hoist myself up onto the roof of the cab, swing my legs over the side, and slip my feet through the window. I let go of the floodlight just as the edge of my butt catches the windowsill and scrape the full length of my back as I slide into the cab. I'm sure I've peeled all the skin off. I'm in agony.

Tucking my arms and hands in front of me, I try to protect my face from hitting the top of the door as the last of me slithers into the cab. Thankfully, there's a seat to catch my fall, but the tank pitches forward as the dock gives way underneath us. I end up rolling forward with it and being tossed to the floor.

Just before I fall, I get a glimpse of a very white-faced man at the steering wheel. He looks surprised to see me, but makes no effort to touch me. Both his hands are locked on the wheel.

Scrambling up to the seat is difficult as the whole tank is swinging back up, bouncing like a ball in the water. *The air inside the engine compartment must be keeping it up temporarily,* I tell myself, rapidly trying to calculate how much time I have left and how deep the water will be if I can get this thing stopped now.

"*Stop!*" I scream at the driver. My voice rings in my ears and bounces around the large cab. Scrambling to get my feet underneath me in the rocking cab, I grab the dash and the seat and lunge for the driver.

His eyes bulge even more and he starts to protest, but my hands on his head and face stop him short. He pushes back in his seat with his body, trying to get away from me but still not let go of the steering wheel.

I shove myself between him and the steering wheel, slamming my full weight into his chest with my shoulder. The air whooshes out of his lungs. He's not much bigger than I am. He might weigh more, but he's underneath me, so it won't help him. My full weight is on his arms and he finally releases the wheel.

With no one at the wheel, it starts to spin of its own accord. The tank starts to dip to one side.

"*Nyet!*" the driver yells in my ear as I turn in place, fighting his hands for the wheel. "*Nyet! Nyet! PER I STAATS!*"

I take the wheel. It's spinning with such force it jars my arms to the point where I fear they will snap in two. No wonder he was hanging on with both hands. It takes all my strength to stop the wheel from turning. He reaches overtop of my shoulder to grab at the wheel as well. The tank stops tipping and slowly begins to come back to level. Not like a car. Like a huge boat that's been hit by a wave.

I let go with one hand to elbow him back, but we're too close to one another for it to have any impact. I can't hold the wheel steady with just one hand. It starts to spin, wrenching my arm with it. The tank bounces in response and begins to tip back again.

I grab for the wheel with both hands to stop it. He grabs for it as well. Behind my back he's wiggling, trying to get out and around me, clawing with his free hand to push me out of the way.

I bend my body so he has the full width of my back pressed against him and bring my feet up to the dash. Pushing hard with my legs, I walk along the dash from almost the midpoint of the truck to just beside the steering wheel. I'm almost bent double, but it gives me the most leverage to crush him behind me and pin him into his seat. His hands can no longer reach. Still he wiggles his fingers in the direction of the wheel, trying desperately to get hold of it.

I won't let him. He mutters something urgently into my back but it isn't in English and I don't care. Keeping control of the wheel, I try to send the tank back towards shallow water before it starts sinking.

For the first time I can see out the window. Our wrestling for the wheel has turned the tank almost completely sideways to the waterline instead of heading straight in. The boats are approaching out the driver's window and there's only open ocean and the mouth of the harbour out the front. I need to get back towards shore before it's too late.

Turning the wheel sharply is out of the question. The amount it dipped before makes me think the whole thing will just roll over and capsize if I crank the wheel again. It feels very unstable. I flex my arms to force the wheel a quarter of a turn back towards shore.

The tank bounces a little in response, but it does start to turn. It seems like an odd thing for a tank to do. It still hasn't started sinking. If anything, it feels like it wants to float. The man pinned behind me becomes frantic. He reaches up with one hand and grabs a handful of my hair, pulling my head back all the way. With his other hand he reaches around to club me in the chest.

It hurts, but I refuse to let go. I can't see where we're going. All I can see is the ceiling of the cab. My head is pinned back to his shoulder. I use my neck muscles to fight against him, but he's got too strong a grip on my hair. It feels like my scalp is going to be ripped off.

The tank lurches to the side as if we've hit something big. It gives my head an extra jerk. One side of the tank feels stable, but the other side is bouncing worse that before. We've either hit bottom or the shore. I don't know which.

From the corner of my eye, I see the passenger-side door opening wide in one quick jerk. The metal hinges squeal from the force. Still I refuse to let go of the wheel. I wait for the water to rush in through the open door. I listen for it, but it does not come. Perhaps I've made it back to the shore.

"Stop!" a sharp voice commands.

"I don't know how!" I scream back, still unable to bring my head back upright. The man behind me goes rigid and stiff.

A quick movement from the side brings a flash of a black-clad body just underneath my line of vision.

It moves in close. I hold my breath, not sure what to expect, not sure if the person's here to stab me or save me. Then the tank jerks to a stop. The black-clad intruder must have found some kind of off switch.

Everything freezes for a full second. The man behind me still has my hair fisted in one hand and is still pulling on my shirt with the other. I'm still staring at the ceiling with both hands locked on the wheel and both feet pressed full force into the dash, with a stranger pinned behind me.

"Are you Brian or Andrew?" the black figure somewhere near me asks intently. I'm more than a bit surprised. I still don't know if this is good or bad. The bad guys might know my name too. I wonder if I should lie, but decide there is no point now.

"I would be the Andrew of those two choices," I whisper through a dry throat.

"You can let go now, son," he tells me.

The whole world sighs.

The man behind me lets go of my shirt and my hair. I let go of the wheel and relax my feet from their place on the dash. We both slump at the same time. He does not fight me as I slide off of him. I edge across the seat towards the open door.

Behind me I hear the driver's door open. I turn to look. There's another man in black standing there holding the door wide. There are splashing water sounds behind him. The doors are ten feet in the air, but I can tell from the splashing sounds around his feet that he's standing in the water. We didn't make it quite all the way back to shore, but we are close enough.

The driver slowly lifts both his hands in the air—the international symbol for "I surrender." The man outside his door grabs him by the shirt and pulls him out. He falls awkwardly, still trying to keep his hands in the air, and although I do not see him, I hear him splashing in the water below.

I turn back to my door and wonder what might happen to me. The man steps back to allow me to climb out on my own. My legs and arms are weak. I can hardly move them for their shaking.

Only now do I hear the roar of motorboats being cut and the yelling and calling of voices from all around. Sitting in the passenger's seat with my feet out the door, I'm not sure I trust my shaking legs to hold me if I drop to the rocky ground below.

The man beside me doesn't offer me his hand to help me down, but he doesn't seem to be trying to keep me in place, either. He's just standing inches away from me, like we're pals watching a baseball game. He turns his head towards the back of the tank. He has no warning that a one hundred and twenty–pound woman is about to shove him over. He staggers sideways as my mother two-hand shoves him out of the doorway. My father is behind her. He half-tries to help the man, but his eyes are on me.

When I see her face, I can't breathe. Tears cloud my eyes and I just cannot breathe. She looks angry and afraid.

"Are you all right?" she asks softly, but she's not listening for my answer. She's patting my feet and legs, working her way up to my hands and thighs. Her frantic patting stops. "Sweetheart, you're bleeding," she cries softly. "What happened? You need to see a doctor!"

I look down. One of her hands is on my right shoulder and the other on my elbow. The shirt in between is soaked with blood.

"I've already been to the hospital. It looks worse than it is; I just scratched myself on some wood," I tell her. It's mostly the truth. Now is not the time to make things worse. It's time to calm things down—me, her, Dad, everything, everyone just needs to give me a few minutes.

"Are you sure?" she asks urgently, but gently. She pats my shoulder and turns my wrist from side to side, making sure it still works.

I nod and try to blink back my swelling tears.

"I could hear you calling for me through the hatch," she explains, moving in close to my face and squeezing my hands up by her chest. "I tried to tell you I was okay, but you couldn't hear me."

I can only squeeze my eyes shut and keep nodding. My mother was inside and she could hear me. My breath catches in my throat. "I was so worried you would drown. I had to do something. No one would have gotten here in time to get you out," I whisper.

"You did, honey," she whispers in my ear. "You got here in time." She climbs up on the running board and presses my face to her chest. "You got here in time."

My whole body sags.

CHAPTER 12

The only thing left to see when the sun comes up are the three tents that held the Jet Skis and a bunch of burn holes on the ground with melted plastic and bits of burned and splintered wood. A few pieces of paper blow around, though there's hardly any breeze. To keep my mind occupied, I try to figure out what all the bits and pieces *used* to be. I see a few pieces of the map that once covered the wall of the big tent.

We aren't supposed to touch anything. The place is swarming with people in white jumpsuits, photographing everything, picking it all up and putting it in tiny plastic bags. I doubt there will be a single blade of grass left by the time they finally leave.

Brian has been allowed over the police line, but Krista and Barry are on the other side. Krista is frantically running along the yellow police tape and shouting at anyone who might look her way. It would appear that the police have taken her video camera and its tape as evidence. They say she should get it back after the trial, which could be as long as ten years.

We've all given our statements three or four times by now. Thankfully, when they have questions, they take us aside and ask them privately. I'm sure I'll end up telling my parents everything eventually, but not today. Not all at once. They're sure to ask us more questions over the days to come. For now, we just sit in the middle of it all on some folding chairs they've given us, and we wait for them to allow us to go home.

"What does a Code Red actually mean?" Brian asks, "I heard it a couple of times last night." He's trying to fill in the long silences when we just sit and think about all the things that could have happened.

"A Code Red," my mother explains, "is the international term that both police forces and governments use for any event where you two are in the room."

"Ha ha," I say, rolling my eyes. "You're not funny."

She sticks her tongue out at me.

"These guys weren't very good, were they?" Brian says. "They were all over the place."

'They were *trying* to be all over the place," Dad explains, "so none of us would be looking at the right place when it really counted."

"Huh?" Brian asks.

"By the time the planes were actually landing, they

had us spread out all over the Citadel, the airport, and the military base, when the whole time they were hiding on McNabs Island, which is where exactly *none* of us were. The only people here were you two boys. They had all of us fooled but you."

Jack enters our little family circle. He walks over to us, handing Dad and Mom another cup of coffee. "It seems they were willing to take the president out anyplace they could get at him. They had lots of backup plans according to Mr. Shiny-Shoes from the airport. He was silent for a bit, but we let the Russian Embassy guys talk to him alone for a bit, and afterwards he sang like a bird. If they didn't get his plane at the airport when it was coming in, they were going to try to get it as it was flying out, over McNabs on its exit from Shearwater. That's why they had the tents, to hide the big guns they had mounted on the amphibious assault vehicle. They only way they could hide a gun big enough to take out a presidential airplane was to disguise the whole rig as one of those floating tourist buses."

I whip my head around to look at Mom. "You mean that thing could *float*?"

"Yes." She nods a little sadly. "They weren't trying to sink the tank, they were trying to escape from the island and bring me with them." She seems to notice my sudden embarrassment about my earlier terror that she was about to die, and quickly adds, "You still saved me, honey, just not from drowning."

After an awkward pause, Jack continues. "If they couldn't take his plane out over McNabs, they were set up to take him out at the Citadel, and everyone else with him. Once they made it into those tunnels, they could have run up under everyone's nose and no one would have known they were there."

"So it was Andrew looking in the window of the Old Town Clock that forced them to detonate the bombs a little early, to cover their tracks—he didn't actually trip a switch by opening the door in the basement. Here I thought they were just trying to bury me alive in the tunnels," Brian says, standing up to stamp his foot, pretending to be indignant.

It makes me laugh for a second, but I'm the only one—Brian just let the cat out of the bag. Until now we'd avoided telling my parents that I was in a building that blew up, and that Brian was in a tunnel when it collapsed.

My parents exchange a did-you-know-about-this-heck-no-did-you look. I try to change the subject.

"Jack," I say loudly, "Is this it, then? Do you think they have any more backup plans for their backup plans?"

"No, we think three backup plans are about all they could coordinate. The rest of the planes have landed and the Russian president is safe. Mostly thanks to you two."

"Yeah," Brian crows, sticking his chest out. "We got in the way of two explosions and a real live tank, man!"

"Brian," I hiss out the side of my mouth, "you're not helping."

"Umm, yes," Jack clears his throat. "The Russian president is aware of your involvement, and as much of an embarrassment as it is to our security teams, he plans to invite you two boys to Moscow once the G8 meetings are over so he can thank you personally."

"Not on your life," my mother interrupts. "These two boys have had enough adventures for one lifetime. I can't leave you two unsupervised for thirty seconds without you getting into trouble."

Brian and I smile at each other and shrug.

"We had adult supervision the whole time, Mom," I say, turning my head towards Krista, who's still flitting along the police line.

"Yeah," Brian interjects. "My parents pick the best babysitters for me when they go away. Your family is always so much fun to hang out with." He smirks and we all laugh.

Just then a man in uniform steps up and tells us we're free to go. There is a police boat on the far side of the island. It's waiting to take us back to Halifax, and we can go home from there. Jack and Dad thank him, but the rest of us stay silent.

"It's been a long night, guys," Dad says to everyone. "How about coming back to our house for some breakfast? I've got a huge pot of shepherd's pie I made for supper last night. I think we've all missed a meal or two since then. It should really hit the spot."

The smack from Brian's hand slapping into his forehead makes everyone turn and look. Everyone but me. I just look at the ground. How are we going to explain this one? It takes every muscle, from my toes up, to keep my face from smiling.

"Umm, Dad?" I say slowly, wondering if there is still a man on our back deck with our house tied between his legs.

"Yes?"

"About that dinner you made..."

"Yes?" He narrows his eyes at me.

"There might not be any left." I can't hold a straight face any longer. I glance at Brian and we burst into laughter.

"But you were right about one thing, sir," Brian adds, looking straight at my dad. "It did hit the spot."

THE INSIDER'S SCOOP

Shhh...don't tell anyone, but the facts hidden within this book are true!

- There really are tunnels underneath the Halifax Citadel, and they really were designed so that gunners could shoot at intruders from behind those thick stone walls. (They have lower ceilings than implied in this book, though, as people used to be much shorter.)

- Cellphones are easy to hack into. You can manipulate them to do almost anything (turn on and off, send out a tracking signal, work as a microphone, and more) remotely. You just need the right equipment and a hacking program to take control!

- You can block, scramble, or hide all wavelength signals by wrapping your building (or tent!) in steel mesh, since cellphones have trouble sending signals through metal. Just make sure the building is completely covered, like in the book. And when you want to send and receive messages, just sneak your antenna out through a small hole, and, just to be safe, scramble your messages, too.

- Amphibious assault vehicles first showed up over five hundred years ago, as far as we can tell from historical records. Today they take on all shapes and sizes, depending on what we need them for. In fact, anyone who's been to Halifax has seen a converted amphibious assault vehicle filled with tourists—the Harbour Hopper.